Temple of the Scapegoat

Also by Alexander Kluge

FROM NEW DIRECTIONS

•

Cinema Stories

The Devil's Blind Spot

Temple of the Scapegoat

OPERA STORIES

by

Alexander Kluge

Translated by Isabel Fargo Cole,
Donna Stonecipher & others

A New Directions Paperbook Original

Published by arrangement with Alexander Kluge.

PUBLISHER'S NOTE: Most of *Temple of the Scapegoat* is translated by Isabel Fargo Cole
(sections I–III) and Donna Stonecipher (sections IV–VI) with the exception of the
following pieces: "Total Commitment," "In the Last Year of his Life," "Snow on a Copper
Roof," "Commitment to a Colleague with a Sore Throat," and "Lost Sketch by John Cage"
by Nathaniel McBride; "The Phenomenon of the Opera," "Lohengrin in Leningrad,"
"*Götterdämmerung* in Vienna," and "Napoleon and Love," by Martin Chalmers; "Correct
Slowing-Down on the Transitional Point between Terror and an Inkling of Freedom,"
"When I see you, I must weep," "Sunday, August 4, 2013, Elmau," "Night of Decisions,"
and "The Complete Version of a Baroque Idea from Christoph Schlingensief" by Wieland
Hoban; "Temples of Seriousness" and "The Original Form of Opera" by Martin Brady.

Manufactured in the United States of America
New Directions Books are printed on acid-free paper
First published as a New Directions Paperbook (NDP1395) in 2018

Library of Congress Cataloging-in-Publication Data
Names: Kluge, Alexander, 1932– author.
Title: Temple of the scapegoat : opera stories / Alexander Kluge ;
translated by Isabel Fargo Cole, Donna Stonecipher & Martin Chalmers.
Other titles: Tempel der Sündenbock. English.
Description: New York : New Directions Publishing, 2018.
Identifiers: LCCN 2017041785 (print) | LCCN 2017048115 (ebook) | ISBN 9780811227490 |
ISBN 9780811227483 (alk. paper)
Subjects: LCSH: Opera.
Classification: LCC ML1700 (ebook) | LCC ML1700 .K5713 2018 (print) | DDC 782.1—dc23
LC record available at https://lccn.loc.gov/2017041785

10 9 8 7 6 5 4 3 2 1

New Directions Books are published for James Laughlin
by New Directions Publishing Corporation
80 Eighth Avenue, New York 10011

Contents

Drama of the Soul and the Body.
Opera by Emilio de' Cavalieri from 1600.

Preface

The oldest opera, performed not in an opera house but in a church, was written in the year 1600. In the following 417 years, around 80,000 operas have been composed. When once asked the reason for my lifelong fascination with these enigmatic musical dramas, I had no ready reply. My English grandmother would have had a word for the plot of most of these dramas—"impractical." Why does the public, in its classic sense (the bourgeoisie; earlier, the aristocracy), erect templelike buildings for operas on the central squares of its cities, splendid as parliaments, on an equal footing with the stock exchange or the law courts?

What moves me in the music is something I cannot express in words. But I can say with certainty that the part of me that responds to the operas' music is not the part preoccupied with the drama performed. Different parts of my soul allow operas, in all their dreamy, unrealistic absurdity, to whip up the surface of my inner seas until a boat might easily capsize. I can't help crying. I know that what creates within me the antirealistic spark suspending all the laws of reality is always two irreconcilable phenomena—the story and the music, neither one more important than the other.

If I can't explain why the SPHINX OF THE OPERA enthralls me, still less can I explain the utility of watching or listening to operas. What is the use of operas in wartime? Ernest Hemingway gives an example. After 1918, hubris drove the Greeks (with plenty of artillery, horses, and trumpets) to advance almost to the Turkish capital of Ankara. They were beaten back. Now Turkish commanders controlled the city of Smyrna, where the Greeks had lived for more than a thousand years. In the evening they'd go to the city's opera house. According to Hemingway, it reminded them of their stays in Paris and their fluency in French. Captivated by the Bellini opera, they neglected to give the command to burn down the entire city. One southwestern district was spared. This was where the brewery belonging to my grandmother's brother stood. He personally regarded opera as superfluous. But Herbert Hausdorf's property and life were saved by opera's power to distract even barbarians.

ALEXANDER KLUGE

Temple of the Scapegoat

I *The Opera Principle*

Total Commitment

He was a singer who gave more than his all. Dramatic renuncia-
tion. He would forget to spare his own voice, with the result that
during many performances he would become vocally bankrupt,
only capable of still displaying technique. His voice was "rough
and gravelly, but possessed a solid and highly metallic core." It
would, wrote the critic of the *New York Times*, be difficult to sur-
pass his *cri de coeur* of "Ah, la maledizione" in *Rigoletto*. By contrast, the critic of the *Washington Post*, while acknowledging that
the baritone's singing possessed a certain aplomb, declared it to
be "without any stylistic delicacy." That wounded him deeply.

Leonard Warren, born Leonard Warenoff in New York in
1911, took over the role of the Doge in *Simon Boccanegra* from
the legendary Lawrence Tibbett. The part put him among his
generation's leading baritones. He was UTTERLY UNSPARING
of himself in defending the position he'd so strenuously sought,
while maintaining a reputation for being "sensitive" and "refined."
However, it was precisely this, the QUALITY OF FEELING in his
singing, that was disputed. The critic at the *Washington Post* was
willing to grant him only a certain NATURAL POWER.

March 4, 1960, was the opening night of Verdi's *La Forza del
Destino* at the Metropolitan Opera House in New York. Leonard
Warren sang the part of Don Carlos, brother to the unfortunate
Leonora (Renata Trebaldi). Following the friendship duet between Alvaro and Don Carlos there was a pause. Warren seemed
to be having difficulties beginning Don Carlos's aria. The great
man gave a sigh. He was about to come to the "O gioia" before

the stretta. Suddenly he froze. Leonora's locket slipped from his hand, and he fell, according to the *Washington Post*, "first with his chest, then with his head" to the ground. The fall was only too real. The audience took fright. At his side, the singer playing Alvaro cried out: "Lennie, Lennie!" Stage hands ran in from the wings and saw blood dripping from his broken nose. Taking turns, the stage manager Osie Hawkins and the tenor Richard Tucker delivered mouth-to-mouth resuscitation to the lifeless man. Dr. Adrian Zorgniotti, the Met's house doctor, could do nothing more than confirm the baritone's death. A half hour passed in confusion. No one had dropped the curtain. At this point, Rudolf Bing, the director of the Met, came on stage and addressed the audience: "This is one of the saddest moments in the history of the Metropolitan. May I ask you all to rise. In tribute to one of our greatest performers. I am sure you will agree with me that it would not be possible to continue with the performance." Only then was the colossus carried from the stage. The critic at the *Washington Post* wrote that this evening at the theater, which ended around the same time that the opera would have ended, had moved him more deeply than any opera could. In this way, Warren's total commitment—his readiness to sacrifice his own life—had had a final, decisive effect on the person who had criticized him so unjustly.

The Phenomenon of the Opera

The daughter of a Chinese censor in Tibet—she was born in an oasis in Sinkiang Province—is writing a doctoral thesis at the University of Chicago. Even after total scholarly immersion in the material, *The Phenomenon of the Opera* still seems "utterly alien" to her. One has to approach this cultural model like Voltaire's *visitor from Sirius* in order to perceive its strangeness. She doesn't see that as a problem, since she is tackling the topic with "disinterested pleasure." She found her path to opera because, on the strength of internet information received in distant Sinkiang, that seemed the most promising way to get to a Western university.

Via the internet (and libraries linked to it) Huang Tse-we has investigated 86,000 operas. A number of simple distinguishing features emerge, she says, when such a mass of music theater works is examined. As for the content of Huang Tse-we's thesis, it contains nothing of relevance to an analysis of imperialism, capitalism or any other manifestation of Western domination; nor is it of any significance as far as the experience of government in China is concerned. Instead, it's about *comprehension* and *passion*. The two never go together. Passion overwhelms comprehension. Comprehension kills passion. This appears to be the essence of all operas, says Huang Tse-we. Something originally entrusted to us is lost. And we mourn it.

She is a nomad, says Huang Tse-we. In Sinkiang the whole desert culture is nomadic. When it comes to the contrast between *passion* and *comprehension,* however, nomads do not have the same problems as sedentary Europeans, whose theatrical conventions inform opera. The fact that emotionally I do not understand this kind of theatricality at all and also do not find the music "homey" or "familiar," still less think of it as mine, qualifies me to make an analysis, says Huang Tse-we.

There are baritone operas, writes Huang Tse-we, tenor operas, soprano operas, contralto operas and bass operas. The distinction between comic and tragic on the other hand, does not yield any genres. Baritone operas form the majority.

A baritone fights for his daughter and *thereby* causes her death (*Rigoletto, Emilia Galotti*). A baritone fights for the tenor and thereby kills the soprano (*La Traviata*). For reasons lying in the past and without any provocation in the apparent plot a baritone of particular obstinacy fights everyone and causes multiple fatalities (*Trovatore, Ernani*).

A bass definitely kills his enemies. (This happens through Wotan or the Grand Inquisitor in *Don Carlo.*) I am not aware of any exception, writes Huang Tse-we. As if the desire to kill increased with the depth of the human voice. Sopranos, on the other hand, appear threatened, even when they don't sing (*Masaniello*). Compared to the mass of soprano victims (out of 86,000 operas, 64,000 end with the death of the soprano) the sacrifice of tenors is small (out of 86,000 operas 1,143 tenors are a write-off).

Fatal outcomes appear to be related to the registers of the male voice. To me as a nomad, writes Huang Tse-we (also sensitive to the feelings of the oppressed Tibetans), such a stationary dramaturgy seems questionable. Furthermore, it is a mistake to make the human voice or the extremely arbitrary Western European orchestral voice traditions the yardstick for Chinese opera. That, rather, is a matter of a music of form, of sandy deserts, of the wind, of the central heavenly body (the sun).

The dissertation was judged unsatisfactory. The Alexander von Humboldt Foundation which, on the strength of an internet draw, had co-funded the *Nomad's Polemic,* regretted the *failure.*

Is Opera Poison or Nourishment?

My parents' honeymoon in 1928 took them to bustling Paris, with their hotel chosen for its proximity to the Palais Garnier, where they attended *Samson and Delilah.* This opera features one of the most haunting of all French love duets.

But how the strange plot confuses the mind! Delilah is a traitor. She has been sent to seduce Israel's hero, to weaken and destroy him. But in their love duet, facing the force of the melodic arcs, she wavers, uncertain for a moment whether it is hate or love she feels. Love's ardor is the main thing, coupled with love's betrayal inciting Samson to a PUNITIVE RAGE, as he ends the opera by using his vast strength to tear down the pillars of the temple and bury the Philistines in the rubble.

What does my mother—a cosmopolitan, a pragmatist—feel when faced with these goings-on? What moves my father, descended from Protestants? The music appeals to them both, but the story is hard to fit into the household of their marriage. Why such concentrated solemnity, when the emotional confusion the protagonists are going through could, in day-to-day living or through firmness of faith, be resolved without complications? Is opera poison or nourishment? The answer depends on the sensibility: my mother's or my father's.

In His Existential Crisis

In that dark time when my parents divorced: I see my father in the twilight, sitting in the so-called Hanseatic chair, plagued by doubts. He couldn't find the right tone to write to my mother or to win her back over the telephone. He could have said: We've raised two children. Against my will you chopped down trees in our garden. Whatever else you've done, it doesn't matter, as long as we don't separate. I don't want to lose you. If a person he trusted had advised him to write something along these lines, perhaps noting down the phrases for him—he might have collected himself, taken action.

As he brooded, he listened to *Pagliacci*. The record played on the console radio with integrated phonograph, a recent acquisition of my mother's. The opera further provoked the depressive part of my father's soul. No comfort for miles around. I loitered close by. I hemmed and hawed, thought I knew a thing or two. I asked when Mother would be back from her long trip. Shouldn't we bake a cake for her return? Then, more urgently: Couldn't he set his anger aside? In every way this was the wrong tone and my suggestions were inappropriate. He understood what I was trying to say. It did not leave him unmoved. But he saw no way out, hopelessness enmeshed him too deeply. When the third LP of the opera was over, he put the first one on again. What use then were my shambling advances?

To this day I fail to understand why at least my mother—who was unswayed by operas and music, and fundamentally agnostic about finalities and blows of fate—had no words at the ready to say (or write): Ernst, let us forget what happened. We'll start all over with a clean slate. With opera there's no way out; without opera there's no way out either. I suspect my parents were confused in their minds that year, and the year before as well. Wartime. The DRUG OF MILITARY CONQUEST, a *pharmakon* that infiltrated people's innermost beings, about two years after its poison of the zeitgeist-suffused reality. THE GROWNUPS OF 1942! Furnished with phantasmagorias. The horizons were staked out by a more fast-paced, robust, worldly life: romantic, familiar from hearsay and popular songs, undefined and thus superior to all existing things. And so in those crucial weeks my mother's mind wasn't focused on saving her marriage. She didn't even have her mind on her children.

Yet in the reality of war outside, the GRAND ILLUSIONS of 1940 had long since fallen away, and my parents were not political, nor had they ever understood the workings of world power. Thus my mother lived in thoughts of self-improvement (returning to the capital from the provinces). And my father, too, constructed notions of what might yet beckon to him in a liberated life.

For my mother to reach decisions in a crisis, operas would generally have been no help. In my father's case, moments from certain operas—of which, however, there were no records in his cabinet—could have caused a STRETCHING OF HIS EMOTIONS, so that hidden powers of volition might have emerged from the caverns and crannies of his character and given him the crucial inspiration while it was still possible for the divorce suit to be retracted. Such opera scenes include:

Fidelio, Act 2, Leonore's aria, "Come, hope."

Un ballo in maschera by Verdi (Amelia's farewell from her child; while witnessing this scene, her husband, who believes himself betrayed, redirects his aggression away from her; instead he will kill his former friend, whom he takes for the adulterer).

Arabella by Richard Strauss (the finale, in which the intrigues are unraveled and Arabella returns to pledge herself to the Slovenian landowner).

Conversation Between Siblings

My sister disputes my interpretation of the scene in which our father listens to *Pagliacci* and fails to come to a decision. She claims our father put the first record back on after listening to the third so that he wouldn't remain stranded in the despair of the third act ("Murder in the Theater"). He wanted to hear, one more time, the prologue that begins the opera, that still holds out hope and expresses the opera's *ludic character*, not the POWER OF FATE. And he ignored me, the whiner, because he was weeping inside.

But I argued: the surging of the music should have given our father strength to call our mother back to him.

He felt too guilty to do that, my sister rejoined. There had been angry words. He had practically thrown our mother out of the house for her adultery.

Yes, I replied, yet the opera, that compilation of such monstrous seriousness, ought to undo those preceding actions. Music lets people overcome all emotional obstacles to recover the dearest thing they have.

To that my sister answered: Try explaining that to a heart in need. We are speaking of two different people here: the real young woman called Alice Kluge—or the mother we imagine, as the case may be. And on the other hand, the man Ernst Kluge in the year 1942—or the father we both have an image of, as the case may be. Only opera brings things together to make a unity.

But then, I argued, hothead that I am, new forms of seriousness (namel y operas) should be invented to recover our mother, to break the obstinacy of our father.

Such operas, my sister was quick to retort, would do no good retroactively.

My father playing the violin. Musicians from Infantry Regiment 12.

Opera Scene that Makes Me Cry

I don't know why, but tears always come to my eyes in the third act of the *Meistersinger* when the shoemaker and poet Hans Sachs enters and at that very moment the crowd breaks into song:

> *Awake, awake, the day draws nigh;*
> *I hear its song in greenwood vales,*
> *a sweet delight: the nightingale.*
> *The night sinks toward the Occident,*
> *the day dawns in the Orient*

In Peter Konwitschny's staging, Hans Sachs begins by standing unnoticed in one of the last rows of the chorus. In the version of the *Meistersinger* at the Volksbühne on Rosa-Luxemburg-Platz in Berlin (performed by just six singers and seven orchestra musicians instead of the 196 customary in Bayreuth; the chorus is made up of all the theater staff members who usually work in the offices or backstage), I cried still harder because the minimal staging, the UNOPERATIC QUALITY, assailed me even more intensely. This skeletal Wagner was by no means an anti-opera, it was Wagner *sans phrase*. I AM TOUCHED, I THINK, BY THE SUDDEN EMERGENCE OF COOPERATION. The opposite of melodrama. Some beloved thing returns home to the rest of us. I imagine how, in the year 1523, a sudden inspiration might have led the peasants, city people, scholars, the nobility (that is, knights) somewhere in Germany to fall into each other's arms (instead of killing each other). Just as the minds of the French were united on July 14, 1789. Even if the images made after the fact strike me as propaganda, my DESIRE FOR THAT COOPERATIVE MOMENT overwhelms my reason. The point of my tears is to wash away the feeble remnants of critical thinking that seek to prevent me from believing in SELFLESS ABANDON.

Rules for Crying

When damp wood sings as it burns, it is the crying of poor souls. When the wind whistles in the firewood and around the corner of the house, the unbaptized children are crying. In the valleys of the North Harz Mountains (especially up in Schierke and Elend), the godfather must buy the newborn baby's cries on the third day after birth. He's supposed to put money in the baby's cradle. If a pregnant woman cries, she'll have a baby that screams and bawls. My mother, as noted above, cried bitterly in February 1937, but the child she bore on April 2, 1937, my sister, has always been cheerful, and never screams at people, as her father and I definitely do.

In Switzerland they say children must be left to cry, for while they cry their hearts grow. In Homer, among the Sioux, on the Andaman Islands and in New Zealand, people returning home are received with tears. That, says Derrida, is not an expression of emotional agitation, but rather a force meant to avert evil. They wish the homecomer well, and wish him to import no evil.

The tears of those left living—those who loved the dead man—burn in the deceased like fire. The more the dead man is wept over, the more water he must bail in the underworld. Thus, in a side valley of the Adige, where an old Latin dialect is spoken, it's said that one should shed at most a cup's worth of tears for a dead child. The deceased see all that goes on for two days after their death, and so there should not be too much weeping in these days.

Deceased children, suffering from their mothers' tears, appeared in the house and pointed to their wet, heavy little shirts. They lugged along a pitcher, filled to the brim with tears, and wouldn't let themselves be laid back in the grave until their mothers promised to stop crying.

My father with Magda Bügelsack, right, Frau Laube (the caretaker's wife, responsible for the housecleaning) and Hilde Wasserthal (successor to Magda as my sister's nanny), left, in the sunroom at my sister's baptism in 1937.

Godard's Fragment

The dress rehearsal for Ludwig van Beethoven's *Fidelio* at the Paris Opera was set for a date which—as no one imagined when it was scheduled—turned out to be three days before the Germans marched into Paris. The *répétiteurs* were practicing, the stagehands and set designers were preparing the scenery. Management had decided to stage the opera, the war with Germany notwithstanding, because Ludwig van Beethoven was Austrian (or indeed a citizen of the world); in the management's view, even Austria's annexation by the German Reich had not affected the national affiliation of his oeuvre.*

---

 * In January 1871, Beethoven's 5th Symphony premiered in Paris while the city was under siege by the Prussians. The proceeds were used to build a cannon which was used to bombard the Prussians as the siege unfolded. In this sense Beethoven was regarded as a Frenchman.

Then all the operas and theaters in Paris were closed by official decree; the personnel prepared to evacuate to Bordeaux along with crucial pieces of scenery. The opera house, the Palais Garnier, was padlocked. But in this ancient building's warren of rehearsal rooms, near the subterranean lake far below its stage, in rooms the news did not reach, the second cast went on rehearsing *Fidelio*. They were completely unaware that the main body of the opera had decamped. Only the next day, having finished rehearsing Act 2, did they find the doors locked. They were trapped, cut off from the Earth's surface, from the light. The group's stage manager, a conscientious sergeant left over from Verdun (kept on at the opera as a charity case), made a mental survey of their provisions and the prospect of drawing water from one of the wells in the depths of the opera. He thought it possible to hold out for ten days. He organized one group to send signals up to the surface by means of shovels originally used for stoking the opera's boilers. As for the rest of the troupe, he thought it best to rehearse the final act, about a liberation. Swift steeds carry a government minister to the gate of a prison. The governor in charge of this prison plans to murder one of the prisoners, his enemy, but is foiled at the last moment. The pale comrades, criminals and freedom fighters united, step out into the light of world history. This must be rehearsed note by note; it is a moment full of improbability, a great moment in music.

Busy with their rehearsals, these lost souls in the opera's bowels were blind to the desperate nature of their situation. Their bread and water were as tightly rationed as in a Spanish prison at the actual time the opera was set.

There was no revolt, not even impatience. The Führer's visit up above went unnoticed by the lost crew. On Tuesday, June 25, with the sun still shining warmly on Paris, the cafés on Boulevard Saint-Germain were packed, rapt Germans already mingling in the crowd. Now the opera staff who had not been evacuated to Bordeaux returned to the Palais Garnier. A stagehand heard the lost brigade's systematically knocking shovels. IT TOOK SEVEN KEYS TO RELEASE THE REHEARSAL GROUP. Not a single eyewitness left an account of the moment when these forsaken people, these Robinsons of France's defeat, emerged from the underground.

Jean-Luc Godard heard this story in 1968.* He always had a surprise up his sleeve. At the same time, he was laboring under a certain influence: his brain was anesthetized by the value abstraction of the revolutionary process unfolding in Paris in May 1968. Nonetheless, a man like Jean-Luc Godard can't be influenced completely, even when a large part of his brain stops working. In dinosaurs the pelvic brain remains intact even when the brain-brain fails. And so there exist unique products of civilization in which each individual cell contains an alternate brain that would go on functioning even if the big brain were suddenly subject to occupation—just as well as Godard's brain would function if it were unoccupied. In this sense, Jean-Luc Godard is the absolute antithesis of the occupation of Paris in 1940. Thus, though his film project THE MOMENT WHEN THE PRISONERS' CHORUS OF FIDELIO WAS LIBERATED FROM THE CATACOMBS OF

---

* For a moment Godard considered a mass production. The chorus of the Palais Garnier, organized by Trotskyites, would have been willing to perform en masse, emerging from one of the opera's basement vaults to sing the final chorus of Beethoven's *Fidelio*. That struck Godard as an excessive outlay of effort. Instead, his cameraman filmed lightbulbs, a torch, a candle, and seventeen portraits of faces from the chorus, each recorded for sixty seconds after hearing an emotionally charged word such as "freedom," "dagger," "fidelity," "audacity," or "murder" (the meaning of the word usually did not register until the thirty-seventh second).

THE PARIS OPERA was not actually filmed in 1968, he did sketch it out in pencil, rather illegibly. His wife left him. His new wife was interested in politics, not in the genius's sketches. But in 1977 Godard, a rigorous man, a Protestant from Geneva, persevered with his notes. The film fragment based on these sketches, one of his best works, depicts in a total of 884 seconds (14.7 minutes, 35mm, b/w, premiered in Seoul, Korea, projected 165 feet high by 230 feet wide onto a highrise, awarded the city's first prize) the EMERGENCE OF THE SECOND CAST OF FIDELIO INTO THE LIGHT IN FRANCE'S DARKEST HOUR.

The leader of the troupe, the sergeant, had instructed his motley crew to strike up the Prisoners' Chorus as they left the Palais Garnier. Eyewitnesses went their separate ways afterward without leaving their addresses for historians to contact them later on. No film team from the Deutsche Wochenschau was standing by, so unexpected was the incident.

Correct Slowing-Down on the Transitional Point Between Terror and an Inkling of Freedom

In Beethoven's opera *Fidelio*, the prisoners step into the light from their jail and immediately launch into the "Prisoners' Chorus." It starts calmly, but very quickly gathers momentum and escalates. The director, Calixto Bieito, considered this form of staging—which follows Beethoven's score and stage directions—unrealistic. The rigidity of all vital functions that had taken hold of everyone in the prison cell could not be discarded quickly, or individually. The director had decided to have a massive metal grid built as part of the set. Moving the chorus members through this obstacle to the foreground of the stage, the director was able to hint at the drawn-out process within which the memory of earlier life is located, and thus the memory of the hope promised by heaven's light. Because none of the sheet music for the opera was available during that particular time, Calixto Bieito arranged with the conductor to borrow a substantial number of bars from the String Quartet op. 132. The music was provided by orchestral musicians floating in a basket above the stage.

Weren't They Glad to Be Liberated?

An SS Death's Head Unit transported the prisoners from the concentration camp to a town near the Danish border and took them to an inn. They were handed over to the Swedish Red Cross (with no concession demanded in return; the intent was merely to facilitate the negotiations by the *Reichsführer-SS*) and treated by doctors as though in a hospital. At first the Swedes attempted to improve the prisoners' physical state by giving them invigorating injections and special rations. The prisoners appeared paralyzed.

—*Weren't they glad to be liberated?*
—*No immediate change in mood was observed.*
—*As if they couldn't believe their new situation yet?*
—*More as if they couldn't find their way out of the situation of captivity. Seemingly caught in a labyrinth.*
—*Was it possible to question them?*
—*At all times. But their answers couldn't be trusted. They struck us as arbitrary.*
—*You mean human souls have too much inertia to cope with such extreme reversals of fate? They need a great deal of time.*
—*Something like that. And everything had to be translated from German into Swedish or English. Information got lost.*

The Scapegoat Principle

When the metropolises of the East were founded (Uruk, Babylon), people were crowded so closely together that aggression built up between them. Only the priests know how to adjust the scales to deal with this "social fever": from time to time a scapegoat, an innocent human being, must be publicly sacrificed. Afterward the victim is canonized, briefly preserving the well-being of the community. This, claims French thinker René Girard, is what operas portray now that religions have been put in their place.

When one rationally questions the magical devices by which the priests (and their operatic echoes) balance out the scales and memorize the new balance, these devices lose their power. For this reason Jürgen Habermas insists that a certain stock of religiosity—like a supply train—must be taken along on every march of the Enlightenment.

A Crucial Character (among Persons None of Whom Are Who They Think They Are): Rachel in *La Juive*

One day the costumes and the scenery burn up (towers, equipment for the cauldron of boiling oil into which Rachel is plunged). And so for several years the audience cannot watch *La Juive*. But its scenes are indelibly burned into the eyes of the young Proust.

The tale concerns the biological daughter of a powerful Christian in Rome. He believes this daughter is dead. Neapolitan troops set a fire. But a Jew rescues the child from the burning

La Juive: Grand opera from 1835 by Jacques Fromental Halévy.

house. He calls her Rachel and raises her. Rachel is proud to be a Jew. In the finale of *La Juive* she goes to her death. She would rather be pushed into the inferno than betray the faith of the man she trusts and believes to be her father. "Let the skin peel from my bones."

The Advantage of a Relationship between Two Women (or between Loyal Men) as Opposed to the Caricature of Man and Woman. An Observation of Proust's

Léopold, the high tenor in *La Juive*, is one of the emperor's generals. He is married to Princess Eudoxie. And so he is committing adultery when he disguises himself as the Jew Samuel to "work" in Rachel's father's workshop and seduce her. In the end he vanishes from the scene. A coward. The two rivals who love him—his wife and Rachel—join forces in solidarity to save the high tenor.

The Opera with Two Roles for High Tenors. Explanation of the Fanaticism of Éléazar, Who Sacrifices Rachel, on the Basis of His High Vocal Range

Éléazar, Rachel's foster father, could easily save her in the fifth act. He need only tell Rachel's biological father, the cardinal, that she is his daughter. There is nothing the cardinal, this SUPREME JUDGE OF THE COUNCIL OF CONSTANCE, longs for more than the return of the daughter he believes is lost forever.

In Act 4 the cardinal meets Rachel, now condemned to death, and seems to sense that he should protect her. Just as children at a puppet show warn the hero when the crocodile is sneaking up on him, the spectators at the Grand Opéra want to call out to the characters to tell them the mistakes they're making. Doom, a very thin garment. Salvation, nearly naked on the stage. In the following scene (the cardinal washes the Jew's feet, humbling himself), Éléazar comes within an inch of telling the truth. Only the unwavering conviction of the Parisian audience—that the seriousness of an opera is proven by the lack of a solution in the fourth act—prevents the singers from embracing one another, holds them back from friendship and enlightenment.

Another strict demand of the medium prohibits a duet between two basses (Éléazar and the cardinal). Thus Éléazar must be sung by a tenor. Singing in such a high range, the Jew can develop no sense of generosity. During the intermission Proust spent a long time discussing this external constraint, which proceeds from the assumption that in the opera house it is not production but consumption—i.e., the spectators' passive enjoyment—that is the "overarching element": the finding of happiness.

The Heroine of the Third Volume of *À la recherche du temps perdu*

After the death of her husband Georges Bizet, Geneviève Halévy married the banker Straus from the Rothschild clan. The Jewish beauty maintained a grand household in her domicile on the Champs-Élysées, built to resemble a noble palace. Her guest and childhood friend Marcel Proust made her into the Duchess of Guermantes (with all the attributes of old French nobility). And so the suffering inflicted upon the scapegoat Rachel in the opera *La Juive* (composed by Geneviève's father) was redressed by an illustrious identity for the daughter. Poetry is the exercise of sovereignty.

A Jew and his daughter
surrounded by hate-filled Christians

Ein Jude und seine Tochter in einer
Umgebung hasserfüllter Christen

Mise-en-scène: Calixto Bieito

Inszenierung:
Calixto Bieito

Silk-Road-Inspired Opera Project
Unexpected Opera Opportunity

In Eurasia's remote eastern regions there are ex-Soviet states
whose populations are quite unfamiliar with opera, and unaware of these nineteenth-century masterpieces' fall from public
favor. For them all operas are new. This was the reasoning of the
accountant and management consultant Detlef Mückert from
Mühlheim/Ruhr, an opera lover himself. His bosom buddy—

i.e., the interlocutor of the pub conversations that made up a considerable part of his life—was Achim Laue, an agent for young opera singers, whose view was that West Germany offered no career prospects whatsoever for THOSE ENTRUSTED TO HIS CARE. Both men were realists.

"Passion's head (the Opera); what would be its foot?" T. W. Adorno

But in Kirgizstan and Tajikistan, the friends thought, latent audience resources would enable an opera renaissance. Why shouldn't BOMBER SQUADRONS OF SERIOSITY (what are operas, if not that?) bring about a rebirth of opera houses in the east?

This would require a transfer of funds eastward. To this end Mückert raised money from investors. This type of fundraising follows a simple pattern. Dentists, men of private means, young managers assemble in a hotel, with attractive women here and there. Achim Laue gives a presentation. He has adopted Mückert's speaking style, one that transforms the *seriosity value* of the project, incommunicable in itself, into a column of premises and conclusions that hold out the prospect of profit. And this opera project's dividends are no more improbable than making a killing on the stock market.

Still extant bridge over a side branch of the Jaxartes. "Passion's Foot" = Endurance. In the rear guard of the royal Macedonian army, surveyors roam from the cities of Greece to the Pamir and to the Indus. In Egypt they search for the sources of the Nile. All that they learn, all the land they survey, all that they claim for the world of the Greek spirits, they have paced off with their OWN FEET. Counted it in double steps and in parasangs. Each man who measured these distances left behind a piece of his life.

Roadside well in late antiquity.

Laue and Mückert, now Co. (Mückert's wife having mortgaged her inheritance), had Siegfried Graue compile an imaginary opera guide. The works it contains, written in the sixteenth to nineteenth centuries, are foreshortened from the present perspective. No work lasts longer than 15 minutes. Six times 15 minutes = 90 minutes. There is a 30-minute intermission for bazaar palaver and bargaining, as is customary in the new countries of the east so eager to join the EU. The intermission is followed by three works, i.e., a 45-minute block, as a sort of FINAL HURRAH. To accommodate the viewers' homeward journey, often into the country's mountain zones, the performance must begin at 5 p.m. and end no more than 165 minutes later. Transport is by bus.

The Aging Singer Stood upon the Stage Like a Barely Movable Piece of Furniture

In all the trappings of her coloraturi. Once her voice had been considered unique. She so loved to sing. That was how she had got into opera: she had risen from being a singer in a provincial choir in Slovakia to become a global star of coloraturi: Rossini, Donizetti, Bellini, Verdi.

Now she herself had canceled her engagement with the Bavarian State Opera. The intervals between her roles had become longer and longer. The critics, initially measured in their reactions, were becoming distinctly negative. A doctor told her that vocal cords, which after all are only muscles, become weaker with age. She knew that herself, that the flow of air could no longer be pressed through this gate as precisely as it could in the past. She changed her doctor. The new one was more polite, but unable to offer her any comfort.

During a guest performance in an Eastern European country, where music wasn't treated quite so invidiously and competitively, the theater's resident doctor sprayed her throat with a medication. Immediately she felt that she had regained the same command of the muscles of her vocal cords that she had had in the past. It was here that she dared to perform sotto voce the entire coloraturi of LINDA DI CHAMOUNIX in their original length. It turned out that the newly appointed artistic director of the Oslo opera house, on the lookout for young talent in the east, happened to be in the audience. He fell in love with the great lady's voice, just as so many others had at the beginning of her career. He wanted to take her on. Earlier in the evening she had taken courage from the effects of the spray, but now, at the end of the grueling performance, she found that her ambition did not extend to embarking on a new adventure of this kind.

Nearly Every Night They Expected an Air Raid while the Opera Was Going On

The grandmother of a certain Swiss clan was a German who had married into the family in 1947. As a twenty-one-year-old *Reichs-arbeitsdienstunterführerin*, she had been assigned to attend Pucci-ni's *Tosca* at the Frankfurt Opera (as the building now called the Old Opera was known before it was damaged in the war). It was customary to delegate young people to attend the opera, an effort to raise the youth quotient in the cultural sphere, which had to be reported to the *Gauleitung* on a monthly basis. Splendid Italian singers, commandeered as booty now that Germany's ally, the Kingdom of Italy, had betrayed the cause. These conscripted can-tatores and cantatrices, including a spectacular Tosca, wouldn't have dreamed of singing more poorly in their exile, in their slav-ery, than they did at home. They deployed their voices because they wanted to use what they had. The theater directors thought the performance was a waste of effort. They expected an air raid, as they did nearly every night while the opera was going on, and the conscripted audience (twenty percent wounded, forty percent young people, twelve percent party members, the rest sold on the open market: no critics, no passionate opera lovers) held little attraction for them.

Indeed, an allied bomber squadron approached the city around 9 p.m. The civil defense headquarters for the Rhine-Main region could not determine whether they were going to drop their bombs or whether it was merely a flyover. And so the performance was interrupted just after the start of the torture scene in Act 2 of Puccini's opera. The audience and the ensemble waited in the cellars in uncertainty. Overheated cellars, with the heating ducts running through the rooms. The bombers passed over, flying eastward, and the opera continued from the point where it had been interrupted. However, the THREAT OF RANDOM DEATH FOR EVERY SINGLE PERSON was still so immediate, and the sweltering heat of the cellar had sunk so deep, that the story's passionate goings-on, Tosca's murder of the Roman police chief, couldn't top what had already come. No on-stage efforts could resuscitate the musical drama once compacted reality had ruptured it. Tosca dropped out, then the singer playing Cavaradossi. They excused themselves, citing sore throats. The curtain fell right after the aria "And the stars were shining." Even before this finale, the sense of having been spared an awful fate severely diminished the listeners' interest in the individual destinies of two lovers circa 1800. Had things taken a different turn that evening, the people now re-ensconced on the red velvet cushions of the auditorium might have been imprisoned in the foundations of the theater, united in the catacomb, the exits to the street blocked by rubble from bomb hits, united with the outstanding singers from the Po Valley, whose vocal prowess could have done nothing to improve the mood of these lost people. Mass death relativizes emotions; indeed, every feeling must first burrow its way out from the reality of the air raids as from a heap of rubble, and only then can it scale the pinnacles of art.

That was the evening on which (due in part to the opera's premature end) the 21-year-old met the man who would become her fiancé, an aide at the Swiss Consulate. Both had been afraid, had been sobered by the interruption of the music. And so it was quite natural for them to strike up a conversation as they left the building. Using her ration card, which she had with her in her special-occasion purse, they ordered two pieces of cake in the blacked-out Café Kranzler, open until midnight to serve the many wounded men in the city. In this way an operatic experience (consisting of two antagonistic forms of expression, the premonitions of bombers circling with the anticipated crashing of the bombs, and then the stretti of the Mediterranean voices) did have a concrete result, something "true and good." It would result in the life of—so far—sixteen grandchildren living in Switzerland's globalized landscapes.

II "In the First Act I Can't Know the Awful Denouement in the Fifth Act"

Conversation with the *Kammersänger*

FRAU PICHOTA: Herr Kammersänger, you're famous for the passion you express in the first act. Critics have written that a spark of hope lights up your face. How do you pull that off? After all, you're a rational person, and you know the awful denouement in the fifth act.

KAMMERSÄNGER: In the first act I don't know it yet.

FRAU PICHOTA: But from the last time—you've just sung the production for the 84th time, haven't you?

KAMMERSÄNGER: Yes, it's a very successful production.

FRAU PICHOTA: Then by now you ought to realize what the awful denouement will be!

KAMMERSÄNGER: I do. But not in the first act.

FRAU PICHOTA: But you aren't stupid!

KAMMERSÄNGER: I'd certainly object to the word.

FRAU PICHOTA: Well then, at 8:10 p.m. in the first act you know from those previous performances what will happen at 10:30 p.m. in the fifth act.

KAMMERSÄNGER: Yes.

FRAU PICHOTA: So why do you play the role "with a spark of hope lighting up your face"?

KAMMERSÄNGER: Because in the first act I can't know the fifth act.

FRAU PICHOTA: You mean that the opera could turn out completely differently?

KAMMERSÄNGER: Of course.

FRAU PICHOTA: But it doesn't turn out differently. For eighty-four times now, it hasn't.

KAMMERSÄNGER: Yes, because it's a successful production.

FRAU PICHOTA: Which is why there've been eighty-four performances. But it doesn't have a happy ending.

KAMMERSÄNGER: Do you object to success?

FRAU PICHOTA: No, but the fifth act doesn't have a happy ending.

KAMMERSÄNGER: But it could!

The Forgetful Diva

In Italy, Austria, and France, the *Kammersängerin* W. was regarded as a star of the first magnitude; in Germany, though, she still had to fight bureaucratic inertia. She fought for her art. Against blundering bureaucracy. She would arrive for performances in the morning to have time to get into the mood. It isn't humanly possible to arrive and simply sing. No great things happen suddenly. The Frankfurt correspondent of the left-wing daily *die tageszeitung* interviewed the artist in her dressing room.

REPORTER: Frau Kammersängerin, do you sing Tosca too?

KAMMERSÄNGERIN: That's the part I'm famous for ...

R: What are your current favorite roles?

K: Today I'm singing Tosca. And Aida, Gilda ...

R: All of them this evening?

K: Sadly, no. Aida is tomorrow.

R: Why do you say: Sadly, no?

K: It would be interesting to compare their different experiences. I believe that from her temporal remove Aida—an Egyptian slave—would know of ways for Tosca to escape from her dilemma and travel safely to La Spezia with her lover; conversely, the prima donna, living around 1804, could surely offer advice of her own to Aida, who lives around 4,000 B.C. Unfortunately, it's impossible for these women to know each other.

R: Is that a feminist perspective?

K: What do you mean?

R: Together we're strong.

K: Yes, we are.

R: But you know all three women: Aida, Tosca, Gilda ...

K: ... and now I'm moving on to dramatic roles, preparing for Kundry, Brunhilde, Asuzena ...

R: Well then, couldn't you combine the advice of all six women?

K: There are difficulties involved.

R: Why is that? You portray all these women.

K: Only one per evening.

R: You could try very hard ...

K: Sadly, every evening I'm still only one of them.

R: Why is that?

K: *Because* I try hard. I focus.

R: And if you didn't?

K: I wouldn't be a single one of them.

R: Well, you still aren't Aida.

K: How do you know?

R: I can see that you're Frau Kammersängerin Wallstabe. You're sitting in front of me.

K: You can't know who's sitting in front of you. If I focus, I *am* Aida.

R: Or the *delusion* of Aida?

K: But then you're the delusion of a reporter.

R: I *am* a journalist.

K: And who lives inside you? A long-dead writer?

R: What do you mean?

K: If there isn't one living inside you, then you might as well not be here.

R: I am here.

K (rising to her feet): I don't believe it.

(Bell signal, three shrill rings, ordered by the stage manager.)

In August 1940, the Chance of Victory Had Already Been Squandered

> *... exhausted, as though*
> *both liberated and dazed,*
> *he seemed to have no hope.*

—You yourself saw Hitler in that state?

—From perhaps two yards away. It's summer. He's leaving the sweltering concert hall. He sat through two acts of *Götterdämmerung*.

—Why "as though liberated"?

—He'd just won the war with France.

—And why without hope?

—He has powers of premonition. He has the impression England won't respond to his peace overtures. He doesn't understand why.

—And this feeling intensifies under the effects of *Götterdämmerung*, a depressive opera.

—He knows how things turn out in Act 3. Wagner didn't need to go on and show the battle with the Huns. It was much more horrific this way, with the gods destroyed, and Valhalla burning.

—And the summer weather, the humidity oppresses the Führer still further?

—When he has his premonitions he becomes hypersensitive.

—Everyone around him is waiting for the crowning achievement, the peace treaty. Happy days for the whole German Reich. Does he himself want peace?

—No doubt about it. The aggressive state of mind that distinguishes him has been set aside for the moment. And he has no idea

where and how and to what purpose the war should be continued.
—That's a dangerous situation for a "Führer."
—And he feels it.

The man who'd observed him from two yards away in Bayreuth in August 1940 was a member of the planning staff at the Foreign Office. He had the vivid impression that in these moments the war was lost for the German Reich. When questioned, however, he admitted that only later developments had led him to that conclusion. In fact, he didn't arrive at this assessment until 1952.

—Then in 1940 this insight wasn't yet within your grasp?
—No, it wasn't.

Hitler couldn't understand (nor did a single member of our planning staff) why Churchill, who had to believe that all was lost, refused to back down. He didn't back down because he expected that the U.S.A. would ultimately enter the war on the side of Great Britain, and that any sign of weakness (after all the build-up in the media) would alienate the U.S.A. from England. He wagered that if he did nothing at all, at most *provoking* the German Reich, the enemy would be sure to make mistakes that would force the allies to take England's side. It was such a haphazard plan that Germany's leadership never even suspected it.

—But you say Hitler had a premonition that time was working against him?
—I'm convinced he knew he was supposed to be provoked into making a mistake. He was cunning. He sensed he was going to be cheated of his victory.
—And that drove him to make the mistakes he made?
—That and his colorful assortment of prejudices about the trajectory of history.

—And so you're saying ex post facto (you were a failure as a planner in 1940, but in 1952 you're wise, though out of a job) that the German Reich lost the war in summer 1940?

—Insofar as the war hadn't already been lost in 1911, 1914, 1918. Peace and success were elusive but possible until September 1940. After that, there was little chance to make up ground, because the provocations that caused one failure of leadership after another came too thick and fast.

Hitler's Favorite Operetta: *The Merry Widow*

They said that Hitler knew the prisoner by name. The prisoners to be deported stood about in groups at the assembly point, a schoolyard. From there they would be escorted to the freight train headed for Magdeburg. The train was waiting at a considerable distance from the freight depot.

It was claimed that this particular prisoner had written the libretto of Adolf Hitler's favorite operetta, and thus special treatment was called for, e.g., release. Otherwise there might be complaints. Likewise you could hardly put a World War I *Pour le mérite* recipient or a flying ace on one of those freight trains, i.e., on the path to doom, without thoroughly reviewing the particulars of his case. After all, the prisoner hadn't merely *been* that enchanting operetta's librettist, he was its author still. You couldn't tell the prisoner's status by looking at him. And so the man (a Party member) in favor of making an exception said to *SS-Scharführer* Hinrichs: Set this prisoner apart. Select him—in a positive sense. Otherwise you can't be sure there won't be trouble.

And so several of the people who'd been rounded up, as well as third parties from the town—for instance an Aryan lawyer and some NSDAP members recruited by the doomed man's friends—tried to stage an intervention: while the train was stopped for over an hour at the Oschersleben junction so that another throng of victims could be swallowed up by the *Ost-Transport*, negotiators approached the guards. (They had followed the train in automobiles.)

Having circumvented the capital of the Reich and crossed the Cottbus–Guben railroad line, the prisoners' grim freight train kept stopping to let military transports pass; each stop stirred hopes of receiving countermanding orders.

The writer of the lines "Strings are playing, hear them saying, 'Love me true'" was convinced that a command from one of the higher-up henchmen, one of the older officers, would cause him to be recognized and freed from his "VEXING QUANDARY." He had a passable knack for piano improvisation. Perhaps he'd find a place in the officers' club orchestra at the camp?

He was filled with hope, though by now his intercessors had fallen hundreds of miles behind. Were they phoning? Pleading for "the higher echelons" to intervene? Even if those overworked benefactors had been activated through social connections in the town where the librettist was arrested, or perhaps phoned from the Reich Chancellery by a subaltern civil servant willing to do a favor (if it didn't take an unreasonable amount of time), it would still have been extremely difficult to trace the lost operetta librettist. The prisoner transports were secret. It would have been impossible to find out which list of names—reported by the transport trains to the central railroad administration—would have to be checked.

The trail was lost in the east. "You'll find me at Maxim's ..." At lunch one day in May, two weeks after this train journey, Hitler's Luftwaffe adjutant remarked that efforts were being made to find the librettist. Hitler had last attended the operetta at the Staatsoper in 1936, but often listened to "pieces from that ravishing tearjerker" on the phonograph. He heard what von Below had to say, but no orders were given.

In the winter of 1942 the librettist lost all hope. In the new society in which he'd begun his new life, "old contacts" counted for nothing. He concentrated on surviving. In the cold of the east. Then he killed himself, before the others could kill him.

"When I see you, I must weep"

Dr. Fritz Löhner-Beda, the lyricist of "Rosa, wir fahr'n nach Lodz" (Rosa, We're Going to Lodz, a wartime hit in 1914), "Ausgerechnet Bananen" (Yes, We Have No Bananas), and "Ich hab' mein Herz in Heidelberg verloren" (I Lost My Heart in Heidelberg), librettist of *The Land of Smiles*, *Giuditta* (dedicated to Mussolini by Léhar), and *Ball at the Savoy*, was arrested in Vienna the day after the Reich's annexation of Austria. Transported to Dachau concentration camp with other celebrities. Lawyers, friends from the U.S.A., operetta-lovers and (to a limited extent) Franz Léhar championed his cause in vain. Relocation to Buchenwald concentration camp in September 1938. Later taken to Auschwitz. The work performance of this intellectual at the I. G. Farben factory there is not excellent. At an inspection by I. G. Farben board members, his demeanor and performance are faulted. They could have sung the hits for which Fritz Löhner-Beda wrote the words, but they did not recognize their author. Owing to his rating as inadequate, Fritz Löhner-Beda was beaten to death the following day. Units from the Office of Strategic Services who went to Austria in late April to search for persons, patents, and depots of copyright-relevant contracts were instructed to determine his whereabouts.*

---

* In Germany, copyright lasts up to seventy years after the holder's death. This means that the numerous rights of Dr. Löhner-Beda expired at the end of 2012. Their relevance lies in the fact that they are connected

IT BEGINS WITH INFATUATION AND ENDS WITH DIVORCE.
IT BEGINS IN 1933 AND ENDS IN RUBBLE.
THE GREAT OPERAS BEGIN AUSPICIOUSLY, WITH HEIGHT-
ENED EMOTIONS, AND IN ACT 5 WE COUNT THE CORPSES.

Appearance and Reality in the Operetta

In 1943 in Krakow, capital of the General Governorate, the German occupiers indulged in a joke. The occasion being a special performance of Karl Millöcker's *The Beggar Student* for an audience of severely wounded soldiers. The plot involves a German colonel during Saxony's dominion over Poland (from 1697 onwards) who makes overtures to a Polish noblewoman and is rebuffed with a slap in the face. Humiliated, he recruits a prisoner from one of the prisons under his command to pose as a prince, woo the noblewoman, and humiliate her in turn. In 1943, in light of current events, this flimsy intrigue was "given an extra edge." The local police commander allowed an authentic prisoner with limited singing abilities to take part in the production. Count Czatorski, the prisoner who amused the wounded men with his inadequate (i.e., travestied) singing, really did hold the high rank claimed in the libretto. Knowing this, the soprano shivered to see the affinity between real-life events and the onstage intrigue

---

to melodies which constituted an elementary and global value through their repetition on all public stations. Is it significant that the time at which these rights expired resulted from a willful act committed under the full responsibility of the German Reich and on its territory? Should the validity not be extended to the point at which a natural death could have been expected, asks the publisher, or should copyright per se in fact be abolished out of protest at the death of this author and sorrow for all his comrades in death, as this case demonstrates its injustice?

thought up in a previous century. She, portraying a high-ranking Polish noblewoman desired by a commander of the occupying power, someone, that is, who by rights would have had a favor coming (in the operetta) if she had surrendered her innocence, was unable to save the prisoner loaned from the real Cracow prison. She would have done anything, risked losing her voice; after the performance she went to the German commanders' box, fell to the ground, pled for the count's life. There was no reaction from the tipsy men.

Later on, the men responsible for the gag were unable to explain to the investigator from general headquarters, who was working with an interrogator from a rival agency, the SS Security Service, why they'd thought it would be funny. The two investigators considered the scene to be "completely inappropriate."

It still seemed macabre to have a condemned man appear in a light opera intended to be amusing. For difficult arias, the guards shoved him onto the stage, where he acted according to instructions while Polish singers sang his part from the wings. The SS investigator, an SS colonel, and the representative of the general headquarters, a lieutenant-colonel, agreed that it would have been in keeping with the "spirit of the operetta" if (utilizing the ups and downs of the operetta plot) the prisoner had been spared the death penalty. An examination of the files revealed that he hadn't been charged with a capital crime; rather, his death would result from the general policy of exterminating Polish nobility (and even those noble families remaining from the time of Austrian rule) for security reasons. You can't make a joke, said the SS colonel, Dr. Hans Rudolfs by name, only to kill in bitter earnest.

After hearing of the conflict, several of the wounded men from the audience wrote petitions. They boasted high distinctions, Knight's Crosses. That was no use either. For a moment the performance (the gag thought up by the stage director) and the reality converged to such an extent that the plot from the "fusty eighteenth century" could actually have unfolded into the "National Socialist present." That would have meant releasing the man, and, if he wished, even marrying the count to the soprano, if she were agreeable (and she was). As such, there was nothing to prevent this happening, nothing except inertia. Count Czatorski was shot three days after the premiere. Just twelve days later the lieutenant-colonel and the SS-colonel managed to obtain exceptional permission for the prisoner's release from the *Reichsführer* SS and the High Command of the Wehrmacht. The *Reichsführer* SS had been talked into it by Colonel Rudolfs, who pointed out that according to traditional Germanic custom, a blunder on the part of the executioner (for instance, a blow that missed the neck) meant that the execution had to be called off. The analogy to the case of "misappropriating the prisoner" seemed plausible to the *Reichsführer*, and he gave his approval. That period saw an inflationary increase in phoned-in approval over life and death.

The Bandits (Jacques Offenbach)

The works Jacques Offenbach wrote for his variety theater in Paris are neither operas (apart from *The Tales of Hoffmann*) nor operettas; they are satirical plays with music, invoking prior knowledge on the part of the audience.

Offenbach wrote *The Bandits* (*Les Brigands*) in just a few days, in the late fall of 1869. A band of robbers, the type we know from Schiller's play, straight from the German forest, are planning their big coup, trying to get in on financial speculations in the capital. Paris has been completely rebuilt by Baron Haussmann, creating value. A key role is played by a Hohenzollern prince with designs on the Spanish throne, which months later will lead to the 1870 Franco-Prussian War. In 1941, the bandits' opening chorus will become the signature tune of the French resistance.

The piece was originally written for a seven-man orchestra (trumpet, piano, accordion, violin, kettledrum, trombone, conductor) and five singers performing twenty-eight roles.

On the eve of a European war, every facet of the impending crisis is caricatured onstage. What gave Offenbach such powers of premonition? At the end of the war, Germany, the robbers' homeland, is united; the Reich is founded in Versailles, a palace in a foreign country, a preposterous location foreshadowed by Offenbach's border station between Spain and Italy. The indemnity which France paid to Germany under the terms of the armistice is already hinted at in the drama. The Palace of Versailles, the Sun King's royal seat, sealed the defeat of France and the establishment of the German Reich, and, forty-eight years later, the defeat of that Reich and France's victory, just as the dining car used for the signing of the armistice, parked in Compiègne, was the site of Hitler's triumph over France twenty-one years after that—this is the principle of foreshortening and dramaturgy used throughout this opera by Offenbach. Prophecy encompassing sixty-nine years in a drama that Offenbach wrote in two weeks. What a Cassandra!

My Passion Burns Hotter than Goulash
(*Countess Maritza* by Emmerich Kálmán)

In 1918 Hungary is humiliated (even more brutally than Austria and the German Reich). Hungary experiences the most radical inflation of all European countries. Rumania and Czechoslovakia have annexed considerable parts of its territory. Hungary's banks and agrarian estates are on their last legs.

Emmerich Kálmán's hit operetta COUNTESS MARITZA is a response to this existential crisis. Humiliation in operetta form, mirthful capitulation. This phenomenon was not repeated in 1945.

An aristocrat who has lost all his land and now seeks only to provide for his sister enters the service of a nouveau riche landowner, Countess Maritza. The cantankerous woman and the cantankerous man fall for each other. The hero's concern for his sister is construed as faithlessness. A lucky coincidence reunites the lovers.

Later, certain East German theaters try to extricate the catchy music from its original context: the operetta is now about an activist who heads a kolkhoz, copes with misunderstandings, and wins the hand of a young workers' council member. It is not a hit. Mirth cannot be disentangled from the misery that gave rise to it (Theodor W. Adorno).

The duet "My Passion Burns Hotter than Goulash" is the high point of the second act.

THE SADNESS OF OPERETTAS WHEN PERFORMED IN A
  REAL OPERA HOUSE
BATACLAN, A CHINOISERIE MUSICALE
THE DARK NIGHT SKY OVER PARIS ON NOVEMBER 13, 2015

Nothing but Music between Body and Mind

At first she'd had nothing to fall back on but "the blood of her family," a fuel that, in the hands of the Sarajevo Music Academy, made her a disciplined voice and reader of notes, tilling music's sacred soil. Now she lived in one of Europe's great cities. This season she was singing ANTIGONA* in the eponymous "model opera of the Enlightenment" by Tommaso Traetta. She trusted the devoted

---

* *Antigona* is the title the Neapolitan Tommaso Traetta gave his opera, which describes the fate of the princess Antigone and deviates markedly from Sophocles' original.

conductor, a specialist in baroque opera, just as she'd bestowed her trust on all those who had supported her career, drawing on a store of openness that, given the explosive social tensions in her homeland, could only have come down from distant ancestors.

She had a right-hand man, a young fellow she'd picked up somewhere and shared a bed with, bodies nestled together in communion, like brother and sister, no more, for she saw herself as a chaste disciple of art. Nor was she sure she truly loved the rescued boy who took such pains for her, though the current of contentment between their bodies at night (without particularly ardent desire) suggested a certain intimacy had developed. But commitment is taken a day at a time, she told herself, and every day she saw plenty of reasons to make this man the sole focus of her emotional ambitions. They talked a great deal; that spoke in his favor. He struck her as an astute, scholarly man, utterly lacking the down-to-earth quality she was used to. Often he surprised her. For her sake he researched the Antigone story at the university library.

The singer's concrete problem was the long vocal lines, written for a castrato and not easily imitated by a woman's soprano trained in the modern manner. Irina had to temper her "bellows"—which made a thin, concentrated air current flow past her vocal cords—to last a length of time that depleted her breath.

She was an angler "in the waters of oblivion"—her chaste lover used such beautiful expressions, that scholarly little brother who grew dearer to her from one nighttime conversation to the next. Compared to her disappointing experiences with success-spoiled love-apostles, he was a delightful soul, indeed a miracle.

Antigone is not a mad aristocratic fighter, her scout reported, she is a HEALER. It's not just the rebellious brother she wants to bury, it's the curse that rests upon the family. But Creon, representing the law, is a stranger to the MAGNANIMITY OF OBLIVION. There is too much at stake for him: all the male descendants of King Oedipus, whom the people still love despite his patricide and his blindness, have killed each other, and Creon has seized power. The law, claimed the companion of the woman singing Antigone, is an excuse for him to consolidate his power. The sons of Oedipus, who caused the civil war, must not be buried, as fodder for the ravens they must be visibly surrendered up to shame. By that same token, Caesar's murderers were defeated when they (and their senate faction) agreed to Caesar's burial (rather than tossing him into the Tiber like a tyrant).

Like all forces of justice, Creon has an interest in delivering guilt from oblivion: by contrast, Princess Antigone takes passionate action to reject the whole legacy of misfortune that clings to the soles of her family's feet. She would rather suffer misfortune herself than infect third parties with her misfortune. She wants to hide her dead brothers in the "waters of oblivion" (or, in landlocked Thebes, the depths of the earth). She knows how pointless it is to keep down the dead by placing stones on their graves. To confine them, it's better to trust their willfulness: trust that it will take them through the bedrock to the vicinity of Gibraltar, where the entrance to Hades lies. The message is that the dead are on the move, claims the source of nighttime warmth, citing G. W. F. Hegel's "Ethical Action, Human and Divine Knowledge, Guilt and Fate."

The "assistant of her nights," her candidate for lifelong commitment, provided Irina with food for thought, which turned out to benefit her vocal prowess. Now he studied the score of *Antigona*, along with Hegel's works. Traetta's model opera belonged to a "musical revolution" that took place in the eighteenth century along the axes of Paris (Gluck), Stockholm (Joseph Martin Kraus), and St. Petersburg (Traetta): a revolt of reason against pure music.

At Empress Catherine's command, Traetta had altered the roles of Haimon and Creon to depart from Sophocles' original. Creon's aim was to claim Oedipus's youngest daughter, Ismene, as his servant and lover and perhaps later on as his wife. In turn, Antigone would marry the ruler's son, Haimon (Emone in the opera). What the usurper Creon couldn't know was that Haimon loved the rebellious Antigone with all his fresh young heart, blindly and with no concern for his own life. In the third act of the opera the two are seen sheltering in an open tomb. They would rather kill themselves than be separated because just one of them is condemned to death. Two duets reveal this libidinous relationship, budding amidst the theater's usual historical dramatics, to be the opera's true heart, in terms of the libretto and the music.

Neither the "simple will of the people" (which Creon instrumentalizes and corrupts) nor "blood and family" (Antigone's burden) is of ultimate significance.

According to the findings of Irina's friend, Empress Catherine refused to watch an opera with a constantly recurring tragic conclusion. Sixty-four times, she said, she had watched the tragedy of Oedipus and his children in Greek or in French, and always with a catastrophic ending: as empress, surely she had the right, just this once, to demand a death-free conclusion. In her opinion, the Enlightenment project in holy Russia called for uplifting stories. Enlightenment without happiness is dead, she said.

Thereupon Traetta devised a scene in which King Creon experiences a "conversion" (METANOIA). Before it's too late, he realizes that the next step in the plot will be for him to lose his son. What is the use of a reign that is not perpetuated in his lineage? And so he is transformed into the most active instigator of the young couple's rescue. In the opera's final scene, reality, substance, calculation, and the amiable nature of the Enlightenment appear as a quartet.

The opera director in the German city was unwilling to accept this version, which completely contradicted Sophocles. At the same time, the conductor insisted on playing the music to the end, that is, with this finale. Four weeks were planned for the attempt to change Traetta's model opera, including new rehearsals. In this crisis, the singer of Antigone ultimately tipped the scales. She pointed out that she was coming down with bronchitis. The premiere must take place immediately, otherwise she couldn't vouch for her voice. Doubts about Irina's respiratory tract seized the team. No one wanted to go without this voice that had emerged so unexpectedly from the Balkans. All this Irina did out of loyalty to her nighttime confessor.

The Impotence of an Ordinary Understanding when Faced with Kaltenbrunner's Men

Puccini's TOSCA was performed at the Teatro dell'Opera di Roma in the fall of 1943, as it is every year. In the third act we see day dawn over Rome. The tenor, a condemned man, takes leave of his life. The music describes the fresh breeze over the ancient city, the vibrant chorus in the living cells of the prisoner's body, and the man's anticipation as he imagines that he might yet have a chance to flee with his beloved and escape this tyrannical state by ship. A short while later he's shot by a firing squad. Rome's chief of police, Scarpia, had promised Tosca to spare her beloved. He doesn't keep his word. And so the audience feels a sense of rightness when Tosca kills him. Many German officers and their Fascist comrades, as well as members of Rome's apolitical high society, had this sequence of scenes etched into their minds, whether they were operagoers or not.

The head of the German Security Service (SD) in Rome, *SS-Obersturmbannführer* Herbert Kappler, did not derive his ideas or decisions from artistic considerations. He was a practical man. From his office he could see far across the city. The police forces at his disposal were inadequate. The chiefs of the

Carabinieri had been arrested, and he was preoccupied by the dangers they posed, as well as worries about how to control the population when disarmed but still dangerous Carabinieri units were at large. According to an order from Himmler, he was to use the German occupation of Rome to move the Roman Jews north. At this point in time such deportations were as far from Kappler's mind as were executions by firing squad. He wanted to use the available freight trains to transport some of the arrested Carabinieri to Northern Italy. Summoning the two most prominent leaders of the Jewish community, Ugo Foà and Dante Almansi, he demanded that they muster Jewish sapper battalions to strengthen Rome's defenses, and also deliver up fifty kilos of gold as BLOOD MONEY within thirty-six hours. In return, quid pro quo, the Jewish population of Rome would be left in peace.

It also struck him that persecuting the Jews in Rome would involve structural inequities. The rich Jews lived scattered throughout the city, and one could not be certain of apprehending them, whereas the poor Jewish population was stuck in the Ghetto near the Vatican. For days the security chief bathed in a sea of consensus. The Vatican offered the Jewish community a papal loan to raise the fifty kilos of gold. Kappler garnered praise from all sides for the "elegant solution," whose details remained secret. On October 7 the collected gold was sent off to the Reich Security Head Office in the sealed car of an express train. LATER, AS IT TURNED OUT, KAPPLER WAS UNABLE TO KEEP HIS WORD.

Embassy counsellor Eitel Friedrich Möllhausen sent telegrams to the Foreign Office in Berlin in support of Kappler's policy. That network of agreement included General Rainer Stahel, the city's Wehrmacht commander.

Then a group of twenty-five SS officers arrived from the Reich: Dannecker's unit. Relatively low-ranking. They came with instructions from the Reich Security Head Office. On October 16 they arrested 1,259 Roman Jews. The action precipitated 288 telephone conversations and telegrams picked up by the British monitoring service. Involving matters of leniency, appeals. Thus people of mixed blood or from mixed marriages were separated out from the group of detainees. 1,007 Jews remained, including 200 children under ten years old. They were placed under guard in the military academy. From there they were escorted to Tiburtina Station. From there to Auschwitz.

On the morning of the raid, Countess Enza Pignatelli alerted the Vatican. Asserting herself with the switchboard operators, she managed to reach Cardinal Secretary of State Maglione. And for one moment (pulling rank), she even got as far as the Pope. The Cardinal Secretary of State summoned the German Ambassador Ernst von Weizsäcker. If the raid continued, Maglione said, the Pope would protest. Weizsäcker replied: Such a step could prompt a German reaction AT THE VERY HIGHEST LEVEL. Did that mean the Pope would be arrested and the Vatican occupied by German troops? asked the church dignitary. Would Maglione permit him not to report this conversation? Weizsäcker asked in return.

Up to this point, the British monitoring service, reconstructing the substance of the discussion from the immediately ensuing phone calls in the Vatican, as well as the ambassador's telegrams, was able to follow the course of events. What is not known is Maglione's exact response to von Weizsäcker's proposal. The Cardinal Secretary of State is said to have agreed that the conversation could be described as "friendly" and left further proceedings up to the discretion of the skilled German diplomat.

In the end, ninety high-ranking officers, diplomats, and other influential figures, both Italian and German, were involved in the attempt to reinstate Kappler's original policy and "save what could still be saved." They could make no headway against the gang of twenty-five DETERMINED MEN who by now had already commandeered the trains; the deportees were rolling away down the railroad tracks in Central Italy.

In 2012, at New York's Columbia University, scholars asked how it was possible for a network of authorities, safeguarded by rank and professional ties, supported by a web of practical rationales, reinforced by considerations of how (morality-wise) these events would be viewed AFTER THE WAR, to find their plans so utterly thwarted by a small group of carpetbaggers (by no means true believers, merely men following orders). The New York conference was jointly organized by the "Corporate Management" and "Contemporary History" faculties. Under today's conditions—the question was posed—how does one respond to the persistent will of a small minority acting on authority of a central command network? How can the majority of the people involved, seeking to follow a contrary plan of action that derives not from central headquarters, but from previous traditions and inertia, prevail and patch its torn network? It seems to me, Anselm Haverkamp expounded, that the WILL that is so much in evidence is not strong in itself. It is an artefact. Would it be comparable to the proverbial "will to power"? asked one of the Americans from the camp of the business economists. Not in the slightest, Haverkamp replied. The concentrated force that works only at that moment, tearing the well-spun net (even just one or two of the twenty-five men could do that much), arises from the energy of the chain of command that reaches all the way to Rome. From a grammatical perspective, such a chain of command consists of threats. Can a threat be met with a counterthreat? came the question in response. The group of twenty-five men, like ambassadors from an alien world, always act as a concerted force, like barbarians, the reply came from the audience. They were capable of isolating any one of their adversaries. That is where the threat lies: anyone who drew his service pistol against them and showed them the door would be isolated an hour later.

The conference went on for hours. The participants expanded on the topic, arguing that when speaking of concrete incidences of a RUTHLESS WILL that breaches the net of civilization, examples from *our* time had to be included. Haverkamp gave the account of a fourteenth-century Dominican monk who marched into an imperial city with seven companions and established a terror regime for an entire year, even though the city council, the leading guilds, the common people, and the nobility all resisted his tyranny. Haverkamp compared this with the stubbornness of Admiral Tirpitz in 1912, when he used the Navy League he had organized in order to extort the Kaiser, the Chancellor, and the Reichstag into continuing the construction of battleships: a small group dominates the whole. The organizational theoreticians refused to see things in this light, claiming that Haverkamp's thesis was *psychologistic*. No, he replied, it is literary: it comments on the examples. Was it perhaps their single-mindedness, the primitive nature of their ambitions, that made the group of twenty-five men in Rome seem so powerful? As the daylight waned, the conference devolved into jocularity. The majority of the participants felt tormented by the questions raised. They would have liked to see the events of October 1943 in Rome swept away as by a wind. Hans Thomalla, a composer invited from Baden-Württemberg, proposed writing an opera with the working title "Tosca 2." A sequence of short scenes would depict the deaths of police and security chiefs or henchmen and executioners; in each case death would intervene before their evil deeds could come to fruition. The majority of those present came to the conclusion that the only way to combat the fanaticism inherent in a chain of command that prevails through the threat of isolation is to destroy that chain before it comes into being.

An Emotional Weapon of Terror

Christoph Schlingensief's film *Mother's Mask* is a remake of one of the Third Reich's last feature films: *The Great Sacrifice* by Veit Harlan, based on a novella by Rudolf Binding. Typhoid abruptly ends the *amour fou* between Carl Raddatz, a genteel horseman returned from the African colonies, and the seductive Kristina Söderbaum, whom he sees riding along the beach like an Amazon princess, dressed in fur and brandishing a bow and arrow. Long after the horseman's death, his abandoned wife (Irene von Meyendorff) disguises herself as her husband and rides past the window of his beloved, who gazes out, haggard from her illness. Irene von Meyendorff waves up at the window just as her adulterous husband once did each evening. That is her sacrifice. And it is the proof of her love for the man she refuses to forget (although he abandoned her). Christoph Schlingensief transplanted all this into down-to-earth, North Rhine-Westphalian surroundings. The screenplay unchanged. A pony instead of the gentleman's racehorse. Carl Raddatz's brother is played by the comedian Helge Schneider. The brothers are enemies. Events are stage-managed by a mother who does not appear in Harlan's film.

Like bacteria superinfecting a wound, in the late 1930s and during World War II a NEW OPERATICITY came to dominate all serious subjects. As few new operas were composed, the effects were seen mainly in the cinema. But Hitler, citing a NEW SERIOSITY, also tells the tale of a "simple woman from Vienna" who, pregnant out of wedlock and abandoned by her lover, embraces death rather than live in dishonor. The Führer applies this lesson to a general who was unwilling to shoot himself following a military catastrophe and preferred to be taken prisoner by the Russians. Hitler expects "existential seriousness," not some cheap sort of pragmatism.

The *emotional comparative* of those years unfolds as follows: suffer misfortune—allow yourself to be profoundly stirred by art—develop such an ardor that total commitment, the commitment of your life, is worthwhile—set off for the front.

Alfred-Ingemar Berndt, a fanatical Nazi who headed a department in the Reich Propaganda Ministry and served as an advisor to Rommel, lauded this NEW ATTITUDE, calling it a "liberation from the bourgeois view of art" and "art as action." However, he added, not every furnace of feeling should be transformed into a deadly missile. If even the soul's blast furnaces were turned into weapons, that would be equivalent to the Japanese kamikaze attacks, which we European National Socialists reject.

Dark Tidings from Days of Splendor

My name is Alfred-Ingemar Berndt. I am the author of REMEMBRANCES OF GREAT DAYS, dedicated to my comrades from the German press. It is I who composed the rhyme:

> *Führer, you raised us when we lay low,*
> *Now show us your face at the window!*

Though I am long dead, those Great Days still stir me. On June 14, 1934—a day of awe-inspiring events—I was in the Führer's D-2600 eight-motor plane when it landed at San Nicolò airport on the Lido. The scene cries out to be captured in words. The first exchange of glances between Il Duce and the Führer was penetrating, appraising. My impression was that they didn't trust each other. Around the two leaders stood grandees of Fascism like Starace and Teruzzi. What I thought was: dolled up like ladies. What I wrote was: "leading fighters in the Fascist Party." It isn't that an experienced propagandist lacks a critical gaze. There are always two levels of consciousness. One from the underside, one for the top.

We boarded the motorboats. Passed a torpedo boat flotilla. The crew at attention on deck in their white dress uniforms. Across to the Doge's Palace. At the Palazzo Vendramin the Führer doffs his visor cap to ride bare-headed past the place where Wagner died. Green afternoon water.

We land at the Piazzale Roma, where the *Autostrada* ends. In automobiles down the Brenta Canal to Stra. The Führer's weak stomach rebels at the swaying, at being transported back and forth. There, too, I have nothing edifying to write. Even in the airplane no beverages were served. The bladder must hold out until the final destination. The Führer's room was designed by Veronese. A thick layer of history covers everything we see.

It is now two hours before midnight. The two rulers "stride" (you can't write "go" or "walk") up the GIANTS' STAIRCASE to the second floor of the Doge's Palace. In the arcade court, on a gallery between the distractingly splashing fountains: the Venice Opera Orchestra. VERDI and WAGNER. A potpourri from *La forza del destino*, followed by Brünnhilde's sacrificial death from the *Ring of the Nibelung*. Orchestra only. Wan light from the courtyard's cast-iron lamps.

The choice of the two long musical pieces strikes me as questionable. I am judging things as a netherworldly newspaperman, looking back from the end of the story. Incidentally, I also reported from Rommel's headquarters outside Cairo, and even in Breslau during the siege (we didn't surrender the city to the Russians until two days after May 8), I published pamphlets for *Operation Werwolf* in the north of the city, using a hand press and my colored pencils (for portrait drawings). To impress the people with their distinguished taste these two statesmen chose two depressing, nocturnal pieces. But the music, like the underside of my observations, of which I note nothing down, betrays the true current of events to which the momentary incidents of great days are oblivious.

"How Much Blood and Horror Lies at the Root of all 'Good Things'!"

Some beasts of prey have limbs designed for strangulation. But CALCULATION, the stranglehold of the mind, was introduced into the evolutionary process by the species Homo sapiens. It defined the primal conflicts within families and clans. This civil war in the earliest human groups, at the interfaces between generations (father and son, brother and sister, brother and brother, matriarchs and excess children in hard times) lasted 100,000 years, according to the research group headed by Lindsay Zanno in North Carolina. Zanno called attention to the eyes of small children; before they can see a thing, their wide-open eyes act upon the mother, swearing to her: "Don't kill me, and I'll be of use to you in your old age or cold weather!"

This, claims the paleobiologist, is one of the oldest oaths in the world. Alfons Hirte from Potsdam disagreed with the American scientist. Nothing that "rational" and directly "confrontational" can come about over a period of 100,000 years, he argued. There are no intentions and no subjects capable of upholding decisions over the long spans of time evolution requires. Lindsay Zanno found this objection unpersuasive. She merely allowed that it was not an oath that ended the killing. Rather, the peace settlement, the *contrat familial*, came about because the children who survived were those with this type of behavior pattern stored in their *germline*, whether it arose by chance or from necessity. Those lacking this behavior pattern died out. An echo of grisly incidents that served to dispose of excess progeny does live on in the genome, Alfons Hirte conceded. This echo, as Hirte put it, must be sung of in the sleep of the millennia. Among paleobiologists, Hirte's manner of expressing himself was regarded as slightly eccentric.

Verdi. *Rigoletto* or *La Maledizione*. Genealogy

One of the briefest bass roles in opera history is that of Monterone in Verdi's *Rigoletto*. Condemned to death as a rebel, he appears briefly in two scenes and is led away to his death. Rigoletto mocks him, and Monterone curses him for his mockery. Thus the original version of Verdi's opera was called *La Maledizione* (The Curse), not *Rigoletto*. The theme of a father killing his daughter (willingly or unwillingly) in order to defend her chastity goes back to antiquity. Lucrecia's rape by a corrupt prince (outrage over the deed led to the downfall of the Roman kings) is echoed by the story of *Virginia*. A powerful judge desires the girl and seeks to subjugate her. The powerless father kills his daughter. The story wandered from culture to culture, and Lessing turned it into *Emilia Galotti*. Emilia's father kills his daughter in order to put her out of reach of the prince's lust. This story served in turn as the basis for Victor Hugo's play *Le roi s'amuse*: the father, once a revolutionary, now a courtier at a corrupt princely court, sacrifices his daughter to protect her virtue. This was the prototype for the libretto of Verdi's opera.

Rigoletto, the Gnome

> *Disarmament in war and in the opera;*
> *the latter is more difficult.*
> F. Nietzsche, "The Dawn"

No doubt the dwarf was more hideous than his descriptions. What was so horrifying was not his small stature and his hump, it was that his skin was nearly transparent, and so delicate that it tore like paper. He suffered from abscesses, swathed all his infirmities in cloth. Xaver Holtzmann wrote: I am trying to dedramatize the story.

1st Possibility: no Gilda

He had acquired his beautiful wife—whom he lost after a year of secret wedlock when she died giving birth to Gilda—because there was no one else to care for her.* The dwarf purchased her in a suburb of Ferrara, just like buying a puppy from a circus. He wouldn't have been able to hold on to her. She behaved as though she were his nurse. He wouldn't stand for it. He tested her. To prove whether she was attached to him for his own sake. All these tests were failures.

She would have been his alone if he'd given her time to prepare for this role. The undramatic variant would have been for the child to die at birth along with her. No Gilda would have been born. The only reason being the filth on the midwife's fingers. The toxins lodged stubbornly under the nails.

2nd Possibility: Gilda as an old woman taking care of her father.

The daughter growing up after her mother's tragic death, Gilda: straight-statured normality, an outstanding sight, an enchanting thing. This seduced the duke. His lust helped her realize that she had to leave her father, or she'd end up as an unhappy old maid at sixty. Rigoletto, her father, would never have let her

---

* She had a voracious appetite. In a family with eight daughters, this young creature was the one left on the shelf.

"stray from him" with a husband. That would have belied all the gestures of affection the girl had lavished on the gnome from earliest childhood. On the other hand, the wise mind trapped in the jester's contorted body couldn't have stood to watch her turning old-maidish, exhausting herself in caring for him. And so he would have pried, made matches for her, then sought the sign that she belonged to HIM ALONE. He got no wind of the affair with the duke. And so the days pass.

> *3rd Possibility: Rigoletto does not incur Monterone's curse in the first place.*

Now we must assume, to de-dramatize the story still further, that when Count Monterone—once before condemned to death as a rebel and pardoned—forced his way into the rooms of the duke, accused him of having dishonored his daughter, and was condemned to death a second time for insulting the sovereign, Rigoletto rescued him with a series of jests. And so Rigoletto escaped the curse of Count Monterone. Rigoletto made sure the rebel would learn that he owed his life to him. In his misfortune, which had not, however, ended his life, the man was grateful to Rigoletto, but after a while forgot him entirely.

> *4th Possibility: Rigoletto and Gilda escape to Pisa. At his daughter's request, Rigoletto forgoes his revenge.*

Now Rigoletto and Gilda would be emigrés in Pisa, refugees, an unlikely couple in the eyes of their neighbors: an affectionate old man and a young woman expecting a child in January. They registered as a married couple. They had no identifying documents. Third-party information led to accusations of an incestuous relationship. Rigoletto could not claim to be sterile, with his daughter there as living proof of his earlier virility. He was thrown into a dungeon and later burned at the stake. The comely child was regarded as a witch. The duke was informed, but did not insist that his illegitimate child be handed over to him. He had lost interest in his experiment. After four years locked in a dungeon, Gilda joined her father in death, undramatically, killed by the magistrate's notions of order and the loquacity of the neighbors.

Xaver Holtzmann's Project:
"Imaginary Opera Guide"

The editor of the Berlin edition of the *Frankfurter Allgemeine Zeitung* possessed more curiosity than one generally expects at big-name newspapers. One of his discoveries was the little-known Xaver Holtzmann, all 600 copies of whose book IMAGINARY OPERA GUIDE had sold out.

—We know what an opera guide is, but what do you mean by "imaginary"?

—I'm asking: What are the operas that don't exist? The twentieth century offers us operatic themes, just as every other century provides material worthy of serious treatment, i.e., an opera, a "work," but operas exist for certain themes and not for other ones. That was what interested me. On that basis I'm developing a proposition or an algorithm. If opera history contains around eighty thousand operas, why shouldn't we have the chance to create about seven hundred missing operas that would be needed to convey the substance of our contemporary experience?

—So that's the reason for your projects?

—Exactly. I propose projects because practical projects are the only way to fight back against silence.

—And for the Tosca theme you've demanded eighty-seven operas?

—With good reason. At this time there are 88,400 police chiefs in the world. AS TIME GOES BY there will be many more. If you go back in history you find a wealth of different police species. For every single one the tragedy of Tosca must be treated differently. My book is a map that composers and librettists should use to orient themselves.

—"Should" or "are able to"?

—Ability is what everything depends on.

Disarmament of Tragic Action

—So disarmament is one of your favorite words?

—It has to do with tragic action.

—What is tragic?

—For Aristotle, the highest form of tragic action is: RECOGNITION at the last moment. Thirsting for revenge, the woman is about to murder the offender—when she recognizes her own son. For the Athenians, this recognition has a stronger appeal than the depiction of depressing fates. Salvation at an impossible moment—that's poignant.

—But you can't name many operas that tell that story.

—That's what I call the opera's "speculative bubble quality." For 150 years, operas outdo each other with ghastlier and ghastlier endings, more reasons for pity and fear. In my view, that has caused them to lose popularity.

—Not under Hitler.

—No. Ninety-nine percent approval ratings among *Volksempfänger* listeners. But that's the wrong project to pursue. What we need to look for is a HAPPY ENDING.

Despite the excessive liberties enjoyed by the Berlin section of the *Frankfurter Allgemeine Zeitung*, the editor was only allowed to print an abridged version. Holtzmann's aesthetic ideals (though he would have spoken in terms of research findings rather than aesthetics) seemed unlikely to appeal to the target audience.

The Theatrical Demolition Expert

Expérimenter des variations sans cesse renouvelées de l'action d'opéra jusqu'à ce que des issues se dégagent du labyrinthe de la répétition tragique: événements tragique à issue heureuse, comme l'Odyssée des produit devant nous.*

For reasons comprehensible only within the French cultural scene, a forgotten East German director had been asked to stage a production of SALOME in a basement room. Sponsorship money was available. Perhaps he'd been asked solely because he'd taken a French course and was capable of expressing himself in this foreign country. But the suddenness with which he was summoned from his dacha north of Potsdam failed to humble him.

This is my view of the material, he said: SALOME isn't the least bit in love with Jokanaan (the fanatic John the Baptist), and we don't end up with the decadent situation in which she orders the execution of the man she loves in order to flaunt his severed head. The situation is more serious. This zealot will overthrow the royal house, and worse, seek to kill her, the princess SALOME. She sees this with the political instinct of all her forebears. She takes charge of events herself (in place of her father, who's hobbled by Roman law, and the other equally stymied Tetrarchs) by slaying the serpent. I'll have her appear, said the East German director,

---

* Pierre Boulez: "Experimenting with ever-new variations of the opera plot until escape routes open up in the labyrinth of tragic repetition: tragic action with a happy ending, such as the Odyssey demonstrates."

in the garb of St. George and escorted by lictors.* SALOME takes the ax from the hand of an aide and strikes the fettered fanatic's head from his shoulders. This is the MOMENT THAT ENDS THE DISCUSSION.

During rehearsals, it soon grew clear that this would be difficult to pull off using the existing text of the Oscar Wilde play (even when drawing on the versions by Maeterlinck and Hugo von Hofmannsthal). The actors were growing indignant at the high-handed director who took away speech after speech until there was hardly anything left to play. At night he tried to write replacement dialogue, and an artist friend of his translated it into French slang. Soon, however, not just dialogue was lacking, but scenes.

The troupe was fundamentally game. Rainald—the East German director—was persuasive when criticizing all the decadent things that had been played far too often and could be left out; he seemed at a loss when it came to developing substitute material, or thinking up surprising and convincing innovations. Was he even interested in SALOME and the ancient world? Was he interested in women's fates or only in executions? By this time the decapitation scene had been thoroughly rehearsed.

The upshot was as follows:

In twelve reiterations, SALOME and the lictors lent to her by the Roman praetor lop off the head of the defenseless Joka-

---

* According to Roman law, lictors escort the provincial governor, who holds the rights of a consul; thus it never would have been permissible for lictors to escort SALOME, who was not a Roman and had no right to kill. By entrusting the princess to the lictors, the governor had violated the law, and later had to stand trial in Rome. The lictors carry axes on their shoulders. This represents the power to take a condemned man from life to death, a right enjoyed only by the Roman senate and the Roman people. In this respect, Oscar Wilde's play offers a confused depiction of events in the tetrarchy.

naan. However, each of these scenes differs in minute details. In night shifts, a music loop was developed from leftover electronic sounds by Pierre Boulez stored in the Centre Pompidou archive, and was used as background music. These loops were interspersed with an aria sung by Adelina Patti, prima voce, from the 1905 version of Salome.

This "plot" (a sequence of differentiations) is interrupted by Jokanaan's (mute) tirades, each of which leads to his execution by SALOME. Then he is thrown (mutely) screaming into a well. Later the tetrarch's palace is set on fire. In the background of these repeated scenes, but still inside the basement room (the theater's erstwhile coal cellar, fairly spacious, with a ceiling about fifteen feet high), a documentary film is shown on a luminous screen, consisting mainly of images from the Russian Revolution of 1905; all the scenes are reenactments. It's the music, Rainald claims, that holds all the production's divergent elements together.

The theater basement was an uncomfortable place to sit. The theater was popular, though, because it always came up with surprises, ways to outwit the spoiled Parisian audience, and it was the absentees, those who'd missed the play, who gave the theater their particular support and insisted on becoming sponsors. The critic from *Le Monde* headlined his article SALOME AS JEANNE D'ARC, JOKANAAN AS RIENZI.

Here ("at last") a CLEAR CONCEPT OF THE ENEMY was shown on stage, enmity on mutual terms. Either—claimed the now-celebrated East German director—you have the plot that's decided from the outset, that eliminates the onstage enemy unmourned and thus sets forth the "event," or you have dialogue. But under my direction dialogue will dismantle the tragedy until no drama is left. What makes me so irresistible, he said, is that I am a broker of peace. Now Rainald was parading pieces in which he took the wrecking ball to Shakespeare's Macbeth and his Lear ("Homecoming of a King"), as well as a prose version of Parsifal which ends—shortly after the first dialogues erupt—with the revolt of the knights and Parsifal's death. Rainald retained large quantities of Wagner music as opposed to the text and the on-stage action.

The successful director, now a Parisian star, had no desire to return to Eastern Germany following reunification.

A Society Does Itself Honor When Small Towns Put on Operas

The on-call theater doctor sits in Seat 7, Row 3. For plays he usu-ally sends a stand-in. At operas he presides himself. Pharmacist Buhmann, prosecutor Genest, landowner Dr. Wischhuren, Lieu-tenant-Colonel Welp and twelve of his officers (all dead just two years later), the mayor—a society does itself honor when small towns put on operas.

Citizens aren't asking for amusement here. They're collec-tively exposing themselves to emotional upheaval. Under these musical conditions, they'd be capable of letting themselves in for things still more serious. But there is no negotiating. No one may disrupt the performance with interjections. But in an emergency the doctor can be summoned. That's why he sits in Seat 7 in Row 3, where he can easily be found.

Six years later the theater, a Tudor-style building, has burned down. The performances are held in the auditorium of Heine's Sausage Factory. The last vestige of "society" (the greater part has fled to West Germany) is watching the premiere of FIDELIO. The cast and orchestra have been borrowed from Magdeburg. At this time all Halberstadt can offer is *Countess Maritza*. In Seat 7, Row 3 sits the doctor. Functionaries, representatives of the So-viet occupying forces, reluctant delegates from factories, hardly any patrons from earlier days. The opera is preceded by opening speeches. The performance seems endless. A single intermission permitting conversation. During the LEONORE OVERTURE NO. 3, traditionally played before the final act, the doctor is summoned. A messenger whispers from the aisle. The doctor squeezes past six seats to get out. A marginal event, a bit of reality encroaching on the performance, animating the auditorium.

Arriving at the scene of the emergency, the doctor sees a priest covering up mirrors, preparing the final sacraments. A breech birth that led to hemorrhage. The guilty midwife has already absconded. The woman should have been taken to the district hospital hours ago. The doctor turns the child around, works the delicate shoulders out from the blood. A tough piece of life. A slender chance remains for the woman as well. The doctor chides the priest. What's he trying to do here? Throw in the towel already? It's impossible to view this pessimist from a different discipline as a colleague.

Within minutes the ambulance has been summoned. A vehicle fueled by coal gas. The doctor accompanies the mother and the bundled-up newborn to the district hospital. The chief physician has been alerted. Snatched from death's clutches, the woman is delivered to his care unscathed, along with her agitated husband. Before the final chorus the doctor makes his way to his seat, past those six operagoers, members of the newly-founded Federation of German Trade Unions, who rise respectfully to their feet. He keeps fidgeting after all the hurry, blood on his shirt, on the back of his pants, he hasn't quite taken his seat when the doors of the prison open, the chorus floods in from both sides. The auditorium has almost weathered the evening's travails. A feeling of liberation spreads, matching the elaborate finale. The artists from Magdeburg have to head back to the buses that brought them from their city. They can take a brief nap on the road.

Walter Benjamin Comes to Halberstadt

Walter Benjamin came to Halberstadt. The Frankfurt-Berlin express had an accident in Aschersleben. The locomotive could be moved neither forward nor backward, thwarting all attempts to employ a substitute means of traction for the legend's train. A nervous Walter Benjamin. He mistrusted the town of Aschersleben.* And felt the efforts of the railroad workers and the train crew were hopeless. A passenger train waiting on the neighboring track took him to Halberstadt's main station as dusk fell. He took a room at the hotel "Prinz Eugen" on Breiter Weg. That evening he visited the Municipal Theater. Opera was foreign to him. He saw a performance of Puccini's *Madame Butterfly*.

At that moment in December 1931, Walter Benjamin, born in 1892, was only about 1,056 yards away from my parents' home, where I was born two months later.

Flowers in the conservatory, marking the birth of a Sunday's child.

---

* This place name was the basis for Thomas Mann's fictitious "Kaisersaschern" in his novel *Doctor Faustus*.

Benjamin sat in the orchestra just twelve yards away from my parents. They sat in Row 2, he sat in Row 14. My parents, who had seen the production twice before, left the theater in the intermission to meet friends at the "Saure Schnauze" pub. The possibility of conversation between Walter Benjamin and my parents can be ruled out.

Benjamin was puzzled by the plot of this musical drama. Here a young Japanese woman was clearly seeking an "escape route" from the dependencies of a rigidly hierarchical semi-colonial society on 572 islands, making a life-or-death attempt to enter the "free world of the U.S.A." It was all about converting "devotion" and the propensity toward hope into the currency of "western traditions." She pays for her emancipation attempt with her life. In this production, by a Berlin director, Cho-Cho-san (known as Butterfly) kills the son she has borne to her lover, a U.S. navy officer. Having cut off all contact with her, he now returns with his wife to visit his former beloved. She wanted the traitor to realize that she still had some power.

Then she killed herself.

This dramaturgic intensification struck Benjamin as "illogical." Here, rather than two individual people colliding and bringing each other misfortune, two systems of a high degree of ABSTRACTION faced off; Madame Butterfly and the U.S. navy lieutenant were merely tools of these forces.

—Since when are lovers logical?
—They aren't. But a musical drama could be: rather than love, it offers information.
—Having her kill the pledge of love, the child, gives the whole thing a drastic turn.
—Perhaps this makes Butterfly less sympathetic, less pitiable, but she gains more "emotional resonance." It becomes clear that she isn't powerless against fate.

After the performance Walter Benjamin made his way through the stage entrance to the artists' dressing rooms and tracked down the director. They went to the very same pub on the Martiniplan where my parents were sitting with their friends—not many pubs in town were still open after the opera let out.

My father and Walter Benjamin, born in the same year—what would they have discussed if (for instance in the pissoir) they had spoken to each other, flouting the social conventions whereby a big-city revolutionary intellectual and a small-town conservative doctor could barely communicate with each other? If they had happened to mention Madame Butterfly within the first twenty seconds, some kind of understanding, an acquaintanceship, might have transcended the boundaries of otherness. Both felt that the Berlin director's embellishment, the killing of the child, constituted an exaggeration: Cho-Cho-san was acting in self-defense. She was no longer "prepared to act," she was "at the end of all acts."

—In this production Cho-Cho-san stabs herself, aiming at her ribs. Is this sort of suicide attempt generally successful?

—You mean: could the on-call doctor rescue her?

—In real life people have no experience committing suicide by stabbing themselves in the ribs.

—If the knife ended up in her stomach, she would die a terrible death. She would have to strike the heart. Administered by an amateur, the blow generally strikes the ribs and is deflected.

—But you want her to survive!

—In most cases the knife doesn't penetrate far enough. If she'd been rushed to the hospital, presumably she would have been saved.

—In this production, that happy ending is impeded by the fact that she kills the child.

—The doctor would say it isn't murder, because she wants to kill herself too.

—A doctor doesn't judge things in legal terms?

—Not usually. The killings at the end of an opera interest me from a medical point of view. How could one help? How to help in a legal sense would be the affair of a different profession.

—The American Consul, who facilitates the illegal love affair and clearly appreciates Butterfly's qualities as well, could provide the young woman with a U.S. visa if a doctor saved her. Then her fate could still take a happy turn.

Meanwhile the birth-year mates, exchanging views, would have finished washing and drying their hands, would have sat back down at their separate tables. For further rapprochement, overcoming the eight yards that separated the tables in the "Saure Schnauze," the two parties would have had to move and sit together. Improbable, given my parents' "bourgeois"-leaning circle and the (arguing) two-person coalition—characterizable as "proletarian-enlightened"—of the out-of-town director and Walter Benjamin, stranded in this backwater. Benjamin caught the early Halberstadt–Berlin train at 9:20.

IL TROVATORE / opera in 4 acts
ON THE ROAD TO DESTINY

III *Fatal Vocal Force vs. Generosity in the Opera*

A Resolute Voice Can Kill

In the nineteenth century, improvisation still flourished. The classic singing style for castrato voices (with sustained, even breaths) had been impatiently abandoned. This robbed the voice of its primacy, the owner of the voice became part of the orchestra, a "symphony musician."

Later, to restore the sense of uniqueness, of something transcending the symphony, vocal force and splendid voices were sought after. By contrast, Richard Wagner glorified the "amateur who can read notes," the naïf with the powerful voice.

In the twentieth century the Great Singing Machines were developed, mainly in the academies of the two superpowers. A voice singing with total commitment was capable of rupturing eardrums, even utterly destroying the brain by deploying resonance at short range. A resolute voice can kill.

Remarks by Adolf Hitler

In his *Table Talk*, A. Hitler points out how wrong it is to make the training of voices or the building of highways dependent on the so-called "question of demand." He'd been told, he said, that there were plenty of Wagnerian tenors available. But then it had become clear how serious the shortage was. Now, in 1942, in the middle of the war, powerful voices could not be trained quickly enough. And that was just for Wagner operas—one also had to keep in mind the music that would be required after the final victory. What powerful voices would need to be trained for their sound to fill the towering monuments for the soldiers who fell on the Eastern Front.

Whether the human voice could even be used as the ultimate weapon, amplified to crush the enemy's willpower, amplifying the effects of the Luftwaffe and the artillery with the spirit of music—he could not yet say. But he felt that the process of human development that had cut us off from the animal world—but also from the sagas and arts that once filled the sky of the gods, the chants and the storm songs—was by no means complete. Technology multiplied human willpower to an incredible extent. He admired the great artists because they could use their voices to dash a person to pieces or convulse or dissolve a brain—but (even in anger, even carried away by the passionate play they were performing onstage) had never yet done so. In that respect, said the Führer, music was a fundamentally gentle thing.

Intermezzo for Big Singing Machines
A Project by Heiner Müller and Luigi Nono

As a "Grand Tableau" before the fifth act of their *King Lear*, Müller/Nono wrote an "Intermezzo for Big Singing Machines." Strictly speaking, this was no longer music, it was the parade of technical sounds that accompanies the violent act of singing when focused in an extremity of effort. As Heiner Müller said, a high soprano trying to drown out the tumult of drums in Verdi's "Requiem" will naturally pee her pants—in the range from high A flat upwards, no abdomen can hold firm when the bladder is half-filled. This produces a trickling, spurting sound that can be recorded by means of a microphone attached below the belt. The breaths taken by the baritone in the stretto sequence in Act 2 of *Rigoletto* are "wrenching." Singing Isolde, Hildegard Behrens fought down a cough during the *Liebestod*. In his Freiburg studio, Nono isolated the respiration that had been forced upward by the suppressed coughing fit and conquered by the next prolonged note, i.e., through sheer discipline. In this way Nono compiled a "Library of Vocal Effort." He gave this raw material to Heiner Müller on a cassette. The aim was to organize these sounds in space, creating an ambient noise of excess effort to be performed in the sixty-six choir lofts of St. Mark's Basilica in Venice.

During the concert, listeners could use flashlights to read Müller's accompanying text, which did not directly reference the sounds or the project. As at an exhibition or in a zoo displaying cripples (all the classic wounds of both world wars), the ruins left by extreme vocal hurdles were performed in Venice and documented on film. The film—with Müller's texts injected via four loudspeakers—constitutes the "Grand Tableau" that opens the fifth act of *Lear*. The desperate king no longer rules over even a vestige of his kingdom. His kingdom lies in ruins.

Harry Kupfer is said to have designed the sets for his *Tristan* so as to hide the singers' water glasses. Nono used his microphone to record the whistling breaths and the noise of the water hastily poured down the gullet. His aim was *not* to hide the singers' thirst. Neither Müller nor Nono was being passive or lazy when they abstained from unnecessary interventions and left the compiled noise sequences as they were. The expressive power arose from their AUTHENTICITY.

Lohengrin in Leningrad
The premiere of *Lohengrin* in Leningrad on June 22, 1941

The collective of the Kirov Theater in Leningrad had been rehearsing *Lohengrin* since March. The premiere was to be the highlight of the 1941 summer season and demonstratively convey to working people the gratitude of the theater collective. The complete opera was to be performed at the premiere, in the same version as the very first Petersburg production; at the subsequent guest performances in provincial cities and in the factory canteens of a number of industrial combines the intention was to present a potpourri, in some cases even without singers, accompanied by the silent dancing of the ballet ensemble. The premiere was to take place in German. It was fixed for July 22, 1941.

As we know, the German troops burst over the Soviet borders in the early hours of that day without declaration of war. In the course of the day mechanized troops encircled the Soviet border forces. The radio proved to be the essential link between the people of the great Soviet realm.

Lohengrin had been drummed into the program since the previous November, the date of Foreign Minister Molotov's visit to Berlin, essentially for practical reasons. The theater had the specialists and the singers. With Verdi the orchestra would have been underemployed. The chief musical director, a member of the Academy, had taken over a seminar at the College of Military Music, the topic of which was the score of *Lohengrin*. Nothing but mere circumstance led to the decision which, on the day of the attack, appeared problematic. Should the premiere of *Lohengrin* be canceled? The house was sold out.*

In the theater the situation was as follows: Singers and orchestra members appeared punctually at 8 a.m. They had fol-

---

* A cancellation gives rise to certain difficulties: 95% of the tickets were divided up between different organizations and factory associations and had already been distributed. A hierarchically selected audience had therefore been organized for the premiere. Only a residual number had been sold, in part with a surcharge, and had disappeared onto the black market, as it were. The management of the Kirov Theater was attached to the idea that one must honestly be able to fetch back the tickets if a "full house" were canceled.

lowed the latest news at home and then in the porter's cubby-hole by the stage door. Now they were rehearsing the end of the third act: the drawing away of the swan, the combining of chorus and singers at the Imperial Diet in Brabant; the Imperial Diet sets off practically en bloc for the east, in order to make war on the Huns.

After a brief discussion, the artists agreed that more than three months' work could not be thrown away, no matter what was happening at the country's borders. Especially such a historic moment could not bear any waste of resources. They were less concerned with the "content" of Richard Wagner's work, than with the staging, acting and musical difficulties which had to be overcome, like a mountain of rubble which has to be cleared away within a certain period of time. At the same time, however, there is also a mountain of pride contained in such work: the pride of the producers.

The director of the opera house calls the First Secretary of the municipal district.

—Comrade Antonov, we are filled with dismay at the misfortune which has befallen our country.

—Not quite right, Comrade Opera Director, a misfortune will befall the intruders. That's the way it must be expressed. "They have started something, whose end they cannot foresee."

—You see things optimistically?

—Absolutely. I don't know any more than that either.

—This evening is the premiere of *Lohengrin*.

—I know. I'm coming.

—I am asking because it is a German piece, sung in German.

—We have not been attacked by Germans, but by Fascists and militarists, who are oppressing their own people. That's how it must be expressed. That could be clarified by an address before the beginning of the performance. A kind of orientation.

—The opera is sung in German, and that can be interpreted as a provocation, if one analyses the texts more closely.

—Given the extremely critical situation could one perhaps have the singing in Russian?

—Out of the question. The singers have rehearsed it in German.

—They must rehearse again.

—In one day that's impossible. We'd first have to prepare piano scores with Russian text, etc.

—Place Russian language announcers at the sides of the stage or in the auditorium and present the text in Russian. Could the singers sing somewhat unclearly?

—From the point of view of the general artistic impression I would advise against it.

—But it would be interesting and informative.

—But also dangerous, given the qualitative content of the texts, Comrade First Secretary.

—Or one leaves out the singing?

—An unusual solution.

—A symphonic performance with spoken texts and banners, which can be understood without a racket. A kind of contemplative evening, a patriotic ceremony.

—Unusual.

—We are living on an unusual day, Comrade. Tchaikovsky's *1812 Overture* is also without singing and fits very well.

—Comrade Antonov, do you know *Lohengrin*?

—No.

—It is a knight's opera with a transcendental hero. It's about the fantasies of a young Teuton woman. Ending with a kind of party congress of the German knights chaired by their Emperor. Chorus, singers and orchestra are deployed as a collective and are actually inseparable. Translated into Russian, the provocative passages are even more evident than if sung in a foreign language. Italian and Turkish costumes, that we have in the wardrobe for the *Barber of Baghdad,* would be best. But that cannot be managed by eight this evening.

The director of the opera collective was new to his post. He had not been involved in the November 1940 program decisions. He had no intention of risking his career because of a lack of political instinct. He had recently been transferred here from Alma Ata and was actually designated for a Party career. Thus he was concerned to make an impartial report and to *share* responsibility with the political leadership in Leningrad.

The First Secretary responded:

—Would you say it is a Socialist piece?

—No.

—Should Richard Wagner be described as a Fascist?

—No.

—As a class-conscious bourgeois, as a revolutionary?

—In his youth.

—Is there a clear difference between Hitler and Richard Wagner?

—A generational difference.

—Will the opera still be comprehensible if it is cut in half or shortened?

—In a strict sense it is not comprehensible at all.

—*Beautiful* music, rather?

—Beautiful music, "unearthly."

—You'll have to improvise.

(Opera director says nothing.)

The Party Secretary promised to call back in twenty minutes.

At Party headquarters in Leningrad that day everything was done in a rush. Mobilization plans had to be implemented; inventories overdue for months, moved to the top of the list of priorities. Then there were phone calls from Moscow, even to the middle-ranking leadership. Most of the time was spent trying to make contact with the border, with the Baltic republics (taking alternate routing via the military communications network and the adjacent networks of the NKVD). Everyone wanted to find out about the situation. None of those responsible had the nerve to attend to *Lohengrin*. But all were set to meet at the opera in the evening. Extraordinary moments have a need of inertia; so meals continue to be served, so appointments make up the structure of the day.

The tram cars traveled inexorably along their tracks. The sun moved rather low across the firmament; the museums opened; the factories were restless. Nervousness. Sensuous perception of the situation, which within twelve weeks would strangle the life of the city, was immediately put in its place by "Party attitude." The political cadres wore the mask of "iron calm." Agitated were the hearts and ears "thinking along" by the wireless sets.

A couple of minutes of exchanges with officials hurrying past in the corridors of Party headquarters (an office building with an elevator) were available to Antonov as the basis of a decision. There were various positions.

1. Proposal: Put censors to work to cut the provocative passages from the opera.
2. Proposal: Perform everything as it has been rehearsed.
3. Cancel the opera and perform a repeat of Rimsky-Korsakov with addresses before and after. Possibly start earlier. Pioneer choirs.
4. Proposal: Cancel the opera, but not because of the content, but due to the danger of an air raid. How is the audience, as a mass of people, to be got down to the cellars if there is a German night attack?

The practically omnipotent dictator of the city, Comrade Zhdanov, knew "Lohengrin." Antonov walked up a couple of the steps to the main entrance beside him. Zhdanov was hurrying to the Commander-in-Chief of the Northern Armed Forces.

Zhdanov's comments on proposal no. 1: Always "business as usual." Display "collective self-confidence." Performance is the essence of the theater.

On no. 2: Leningrad is not fighting against Germany, but against the Fascist aggressors, who first of all subjugated Germany, a predatory horde, therefore, facing their destruction. "We don't even acknowledge it as war."

On no. 3: Is *Lohengrin* about a predatory horde? No, not at all. What, therefore, is the position of "collective Soviet self-confidence"? — It is precisely on this day that we shall perform *Lohengrin*, and in German. You ask whether it can be broadcast: it will confuse the enemy if German voices resound from the wireless sets of the Soviet Union.

To Antonov Leningrad's boss seemed "drunk with haste." Neglected Five-Year Plans were to be made up within days. Antonov had nothing but these words left floating in the stairwell, without a memo, without witnesses. After this ORIENTATION his doubts were, if anything, greater.

In the early evening the network of the Leningrad hierarchies gathered together in the opera foyer. Field telephone lines had been laid for the Party leaders and, indeed, as the audience took their seats they saw the Party cadres telephoning, discussing things inside and around the auditorium, a coming and going that reached into the boxes.

Seven speakers had been distributed around the stalls. They had megaphones. Each standing at a lectern, they read Wagner's texts and stage directions in Russian in synchrony with the musical goings-on. There were three female prompters and four actors chosen from the theater company whose dark and light voices seemed to match the characterization of Ortrud, Elsa, Lohengrin, Heinrich I, and Telramund. The speakers were instructed to whisper loudly.*

The backdrop for the first and last acts was changed. Decor from the May 1st ceremonies had been brought from props and the back of the stage rigged out with flags and topical slogans. To reduce the risk that could result from an air raid, the "private" second act was omitted. First and third acts produced in a vague sense a "more political" version. The abridgment "condensed" the opera into a "demonstration of the city of Leningrad's will to survive." That was announced.

Antonov, who had saved the evening, was hearing the music for the first time in his life. He was already won over during the prelude and congratulated himself on the idea of having the corps de ballet lay flowers in front of the flags and posters with slogans, before the chorus and singers entered. The languidly progressing, gentle music of the strings and the pattering of the ballet shoes on the stage seemed to him expressive of a "realistic working class Party line." An appropriate evening for the beginning of a war which no one here had wanted. He found the megaphone-enhanced speaking voices splendid, as they inserted the scraps of words between the music and the singing, so that the listeners always had something vague to think about; this vagueness, thought Antonov, became filled with the events of the day, so that the fragmentary memory of the radio broadcasts

---

* The loud whispering was suitably amplified by the megaphones. It turned out that the whispered text prevails over singers and orchestra and is less disruptive than "actorly speech" when heard from amid the audience in the stalls. The whispering gets rid of the traces of theatrical training as well as of the realism of everyday language. Both are of advantage to the peculiarity of the Wagner texts.

of powerful marches and songs also entered into Richard Wagner's music. The audience, essentially factory employees, Party members, and also a few military people, appeared both happy and comforted to be together.

That same night the orchestra members were armed as a special unit and marched off to the front. The opera was closed. Within an hour everything not directly necessary for the struggle was canceled. The Socialist generosity Antonov had had in mind up to the beginning of the opera ("magnanimity as intellectual weapon") was over and done with. To Antonov it seemed, however, a sign of the future victory that the war was not immediately able to divide everyone and everything into friend and foe, but that at least for a short time, i.e., for one day, an exceptional capacity for differentiation could be worked out, coming to life for one evening: a space between aggression and art.

Götterdämmerung in Vienna
(for Heiner Müller)

> *The way that the twentieth century appropriates music.*
> Gerard Schlesinger, *Cahiers du Cinéma*

> *Whatever is not broken, cannot be saved.*
> H. Müller, *Cruel Beauty of an Opera Recording*

In March 1945 the metropolis of Vienna was surrounded by Soviet shock troops. Only to the north and northwest was there still a land link to the Reich. At this moment the Gauleiter and Reich Defense Commissar Baldur von Schirach, ruler of the city, ordered a final gala performance of *Götterdämmerung*. In the hopeless situation of the city and the Reich, the despair of the Nibelungs (but also the hope of return contained in the final chords), composed by Richard Wagner, was to be broadcast on all the transmitters of the southeast, insofar as these were in German hands. "Even if the Reich comes to be destroyed, music still remains to us." The opera house, shut down and bolted and barred on all sides since October, was opened up again. Orchestra members were brought from the fronts to the Gau capital. On the evening before the dress rehearsal (with orchestra and costumes, but without Valhalla in flames, the final rehearsal was then to be recorded and broadcast by the radio station, a premiere was dispensed with), U.S. squadrons flying from Italy to Vienna bombed the city center. THE OPERA BURNED OUT.

Now the opera rehearsed in groups, split up between various air-raid shelters in the city. The left side of the orchestra worked in five groups in cellars on the Ringstrasse; the right side including timpani in four cellars in Kärntner Strasse as well as on side streets. The singers were distributed between the orchestra groups. They were supposed to try to sing "like instruments." They could not be positioned in relation to one another, since after all they were singing in different cellars. The conductor sat in the wine cellar of a restaurant, at first without any connection, but was soon linked to all the cellars by FIELD TELEPHONE.

Artillery shells exploding in the vicinity. During rehearsals there were two daylight raids by U.S. air force units. Defending heavy artillery was dug in nearby and was finding the range of Soviet long-distance guns. Infantrymen and railway workers had been allocated to the rehearsing music sections as runners. The information delivered in this way was supplemented by field telephones, which not only linked the conductor with the orchestra sections but also linked them with one another. The sound of the rehearsing neighbors was transmitted over the lines and amplified by loudspeakers. In broad outline, therefore, the musicians could register the sounds of the musicians playing separately from them, while they themselves rehearsed the parts of the score for which they were responsible. Later the conductor hurried from cellar to cellar giving instructions on the spot. THERE ARE COMPLETELY DIFFERENT CONSIDERATIONS TO BE TAKEN INTO ACCOUNT, HE SAID, THAN AT A DRESS REHEARSAL WHERE EVERYONE IS PRESENT.

A different sound was also produced. The noise of the final battle for Vienna could not be filtered out, the orchestra fragments produced no unified sound. Since the Vienna bridges were threatened, the commanding officer, Colonel-General Rendulic, passed on a warning to the staff of the Reich Defense Commissar. The evacuation of the singers and orchestra members to the west of Austria must be given priority, if they were to be saved. Consequently it was impossible to wait for the dress rehearsal; instead something had to be improvised. At that the Reich Defense Commissar, a young man, ordered that the wireless recordings of the sound worked out thus far were to be made immediately, i.e., the very same day. The radio engineers therefore began to record the "fragments" of *Götterdämmerung* at 11:30 a.m. with the first scene of the third act (Siegfried and the Rhine Maidens).

The opera was taken through to the end of the third scene of the third act. Acts one and two of the music drama were to follow. The intention was to patch it all together at the radio station, or instead, once the original tapes had been flown out of Vienna, to fit everything together and broadcast the work without interruption from the Reich Broadcasting Station Salzburg.

BY CHANCE, however, 9,800 feet of 35 mm Agfa color film were still stored in Vienna. Lieutenant-Colonel of the Staff Gerd Jänicke, who had concentrated the four propaganda companies under his command in the besieged Vienna area, had the firm intention of filming the tragedy of this city. Now his decision took solid shape. He ordered the orchestra's achievement to be captured on film and in sound, and without consideration for camera noise, since a "blimp"* was not available. To Jänicke the shooting of the last act of *Götterdämmerung* seemed the crowning conclusion of his seven years of devoted work as chronicler and propagandist. There was nothing to be glossed over; instead it was about documenting a perseverance that maintained what would not be destroyed with the German Reich: German music.

The third act and parts of the first act were recorded with five cameras, each with sound recording apparatus. Antiaircraft searchlights were set up as lamps: they shone on the cellar walls and gave a bright, indirect light. For the complete impression robust improvisation was necessary: thus the singers and orchestra sections in other cellars not being recorded by the film teams were included in the performance via radio telephone and stored on 17.5 mm audiotape; later they were cut into the mix. In the first scene of the third act an effort had still been made to achieve an overall sound, but after that, in scenes 2 and 3 of Act 3, there was a shift to presenting the fragments to the listeners one after the other. In the film these scenes were heard and seen nine times in succession: each time a noisy section of the orchestra played the score that it was rehearsing in its cellar.

The civilian management of Radio Salzburg displayed the institutional cowardice typical of broadcasting corporations. It considered that the sound recording of *Götterdämmerung*, assembled from a number of unequal parts, could not be broadcast for "reasons of quality." Telephone calls from the staff of the Reich Defense Commissar were unable to persuade it to alter its judgement. As if in the present situation of the Reich what matters is some kind of peacetime recording quality! said Captain von Tuscheck, the officer on Schirach's staff responsible for the operation. But the civilian management in Salzburg remained adamant. It

---

* Muffling protective casing, which soundproofs the loud sound of the camera motor.

transmitted a prerecorded version of Act 3 of *Götterdämmerung* and after that only marches until the surrender of Salzburg.

Lieutenant-Colonel Jänicke's propaganda units, on the other hand, safeguarded the undeveloped negative and sound materials in a garage in Vienna's Hofburg Palace. The intention was to transport them to Oslo or Narvik on one of the last aircraft to fly out of Vienna. There was a film laboratory in the north. The recording was to be snatched from the enemy's grasp, presenting a last message from the fighting Reich. In this war, unlike 1918, the bodies, the tanks, the cities were smashed, but the spirit remained intact. Theoretically, said Jänicke, final victory is possible, even if all means of defense were destroyed, through will and intellectual weapons alone. This was true above all by means of music.

The transport of the *Götterdämmerung* film could no longer take place, because no vehicles were available to take it to the airport.

Meanwhile night had fallen. The musicians climbed out into the open air from their cellars. Infantry NCO's led them through the city center, which was under unsighted artillery fire. They reached the buses and were driven out of Vienna (the last from the closing pocket). The morning found them in rural surroundings. They were distributed among farms in the neighborhood of Linz and a few days later were arrested by American troops.

The cans of film in the garage, still properly labelled, were secured by Soviet officers and forgotten. A Georgian colonel, who spoke French, handed the pile over to a Tartar lieutenant colonel, who could read the German writing (which admittedly he only revealed to trustworthy friends, not the Georgian colleague). The lieutenant colonel had the undeveloped film material brought to his garrison town, Sochi, where it was stored in the municipal museum's basement for decades.

In 1991, after the collapse of the Imperium, a young composer, who described himself as Luigi Nono's representative for Russia, discovered this stock. He was following a lead in a specialist music periodical published in the Crimea, which has its own internet page. Without ever having seen any of the material or even being familiar with the place where it was stored, the young man organized its dispatch to a film studio in Hungary, where he had the material developed. The rolls of positive film were brought to Venice. The intention was to present the soundtrack in St. Mark's Cathedral on the tenth anniversary of Luigi Nono's death.

A film editor and assistant of J. L. Godard, who had heard of this transfer, insisted, however, on being allowed to synch the materials in the laboratories of the Cinétype Studios in Paris and screened the 9,800 feet of film, both visual and audio material, to a group of staff members of *Cahiers du Cinéma* and the *Cinémathèque*.*

The effect of the material (after fifty years storage) was "enchanting," writes Gerard Schlesinger in *Cahiers du Cinéma*.

The 35mm film material had first of all been developed through self-exposure, causing outlines and discoloration, and then the unexposed negatives had once again been developed in the lab, so that shadows and echoes were superimposed on the outlines and discoloration. Parts of the material are scratched and, contrary to one of the theses of Walter Benjamin, have acquired a *unique* character because of the damage. "The soundtrack," writes

---

* Synch = Picture and sound are synchronized in the editing room. She had edited the 17.5 perforated tapes with their curious sound fragments into a coherent version. Otherwise it would not have been possible to synch the image sections and the much longer sound sections, she said. She had followed the descriptions noted on the tins with the sound tapes. She didn't speak any German herself, but had an acquaintance at the Paris Goethe Institute, with whom she occasionally slept.

Schlesinger, "displays a 'cruel beauty' or 'something like strength of character.'" Richard Wagner should *always* be "fragmented" in this way. An authentic noise trace records the sound of the camera and the artillery and bomb detonations. This original sound, the "being-in-the-middle-of-it," puts a rhythm to Wagner's music and turns it from a phrase of the nineteenth century into the PROPERTY of the twentieth century.

In some images the camera and the tripod as well as the sound apparatus are visible. The "interventions of the female prompters have the high tone color of the Ufa sound films. The high pitch of the voices in the sound films of the time, therefore, appears to be not only a result of the speech training of the actors, but also of the rules of the sound recording."

It would be a mistake, according to Schlesinger, to mix the sound fragments. Unlike the original recording, that would result in a POOR OVERALL SOUND. The mixing of the sound sections only documented the *intention* of those shooting the film, not, however, what they *did*: here it was a matter of an inspired discovery, that is, of the BEAUTY OF FRAGMENTS.

Thanks to the intervention of *Cahiers du Cinéma* the 9,800 feet of film and the surplus sound fragments are consequently shown as a total of one hundred and two separate pieces. Each picture section has been allocated only one soundtrack. Where pictures are missing, a concert without images is heard in the cinema. At the suggestion of *Cahiers du Cinéma* Nono's representative included the work in the composer's catalog. A successful work is not what an individual's mind thinks up as scores, but whatever treasures of music he finds and preserves. Indeed, it is an art to get hold of such a treasure. I would not have been able to think up a telephone booth voice, says Nono's representative, and certainly not one possessing such powers of expression. This is a unique audiovisual work of the twentieth century. "Property is the luck of finding such a treasure once in a lifetime."

Picture description:

They were sitting at the back of the projection room in the labs of the Cinétyp Paris company. They were supposed to collaborate on logging the dailies (with picture and sound synch). It was a question of quality control.

—You can see the light bulbs shining on the cellar ceiling as well as the torches shining on the music stands.
—Apart from that the walls are bright.
—The flashlights are replaced from time to time.
—When the batteries have to be changed. You can see that some of the flashlights are already growing weaker.
—The faces are in the shadows.
—Yes, but the forceful movement of the musicians moves the shadows, so that something "spiritual" keeps the room in motion, the suggestion of "industrious figures."
—Clouds of dust floating past the lamps. Those are shells exploding.
—Or bombs.
—Yes.
—Dust has to be wiped from the instruments. More often than at rehearsals in the opera house. Look here: the brass group, taking a break to clean their instruments. Mixed dust and spittle.
—Now this group has to jump to bar 486?
—Exactly. So now it's synchronous with the strings and the individual singer again, whom we hear, amplified by loudspeaker, from the neighboring cellar via the radiotelephone.
—Would you say it sounds "croaky"?
—Simply how a piece of Wehrmacht communications equipment sounds. Listen, the artillery sounds tinny, too, in the recording, i.e., in terms of sound quality it's a mistake.
—Here three of the seven orchestra sections part company.

—Just as in the churches of the High Middle Ages. The notes wander around the space. There's no "harmony."

—But with the best will in the world it's impossible to say that the radio telephones—and here you see only one telephone connection with loudspeakers directly linked by wire—produce a *qualified space*. It's more of an anti-cathedral.

—But the imagination of a space works all the better.

—Why better?

—Think of the actual situation. At any moment one of the other musicians' cellars (or one's own) can be hit and collapse. Then you would hear only the sound of the catastrophe. The actual situation determines the imagination.

—It is not the sound of a space, but of a cage?

—Of course: the group sound of many spaces. A kind of *Lebensraum*, and music has for once arrived in real conditions. That is achieved not by a symphony orchestra setting up in a factory, and acting as if that is a place for symphony concerts. The factory is made unreal, and that is not a way of making music real. Here, however, in the emergency of besieged Vienna, there arises a new kind of sound space of real music: the resurrection of music out of the spirit of contemporary history. The spaces are the message. In the chatter of musical notes I imagine the starry sky. Something pure, clear.

—And you think Richard Wagner had that in mind?

—That's what I assume.

—But he doesn't belong in the twentieth century.

—A timeless genius is used to picking up everything musically valuable. Do you hear that? That's brass group 4 with a kettledrum and three cellos from the right-hand side of the orchestra. It sounds very like Giacomo Meyerbeer, *La Juive*, Act V, scene I. Wagner has it from *there*, and here it returns to the right space: back to Meyerbeer. Music cannot be expropriated.

—It sounds "interesting."

—"Captivating." That's the right word.

—It's dark here.

—Yes, a series of near hits has destroyed the electric cable. Some of the flashlights are lying on the floor. Look, infantrymen running up the cellar stairs to repair the electrical connections. You can see something with the help of the pocket lamps, which are now being attached to the music stands again. And there, candlelight, a candelabra with twelve candles as general light. Useless for reading notes at the individual stands, but comforting for the room as a whole. There's the conductor coming in. He whispers instructions to the first violin and to the two singers. He's carrying a basket with twelve new flashlights and provisions.

—The other cellars know nothing about the temporary loss of this group of musicians?

—They do. They're told by radio. On the left there you see an army radio operator. There are also female prompters distributed between the cellars. This one here has a Hungarian accent and has been borrowed from the operetta.

—Would it not have been a better idea to play *Rheingold* rather than *Götterdämmerung*? It would have been a hopeful beginning. Better propaganda than a drama of doom.

—The people in Vienna were no longer prone to exaggeration and couldn't lie any more either. The people who organized this were desperate and full of grief.

—An unconscious work of art with a claim to truth?

—To the extent that every intention came to nothing, and that something else was produced that no single person wanted. No one ever imagined that air-raid shelters could become art workshops.

—Difficult to believe.

—A find. The main achievement consisted in making this find in the cellars of the museum in Sochi.

—Do you think there are many more such finds to be made in the world?
—Many. You have to assume, that for six thousand years now, something is always lying hidden somewhere or has been lost.

In the Last Year of His Life

In the last year of his life, Christoph Schlingensief—who was being bombarded with offers and whom the director of the Bavarian State Opera had asked to direct *Tristan* as his next-but-one project—began planning a production of Wagner's *Ring Cycle*. He was only prepared to take on staging the work if he was allowed to perform the sequence of its operas in reverse: beginning with the GÖTTERDÄMMERUNG, then SIEGFRIED, then the VALKYRIE and finally the RHEINGOLD. At the end, however (since the RHEINGOLD is short), "dreamlike" renditions of the TODESVERKÜNDIGUNG from the VALKYRIE and SIEGFRIED'S DEATH from the GÖTTERDÄMMERUNG would be repeated concertante. And really SIEGFRIED'S DEATH should be heard first, and only then the TODESVERKÜNDIGUNG. The ending should be composed of a moment of great anticipation and complete openness of action. He was convinced that this sequence—in sensory terms, utterly satisfying—would become the established one for Wagner's *Ring*. The waves of the Rhine, which overflow their banks in the third act of the GÖTTERDÄMMERUNG, and the scene of Valhalla in flames should visually transform themselves into the star masses of a galaxy, so that it becomes clear that Wagner is not only describing the drama of a race of gods and their great fall from power, but that this work is also about the history of time on earth, namely 4.5 billion years, which moves backward as well as forward, and which is not an arrow but a circle, and which, like the serpent, inhabits Mount Kailash. Wagner was definitely a Buddhist, and merely concealed this in a private religion decked out with the trappings of Christianity. Schlingensief was in a hurry. He sensed that his body was in revolt. He was counting his days.

Napoleon and Love

Rossini composed two operas (at once) for the 1820 season: *The Return of Odysseus* and *The Italian Girl in Minsk*. The count sat in one of the boxes of the Opera, accompanied by his pretty daughter, whom an impartial observer could have taken for his lover; in another box, without greeting the count, sat Marie and her second husband (the first marriage had been dissolved). She had not, like the wife of Ulysses, waited twenty years for a husband believed dead, nor had she bravely defended his property against the suitors. The count had not shot the stranger, who had besieged and conquered his wife: a world of irresolutions. All watched their own fate, which filled the stage, inimitable and confirming the muteness of their private feelings. Marie remained paralyzed. Only Sophie wept bitterly, because she believed she had to express the emotion of her beloved father.

Resolution: It has occurred en masse ever since Napoleon's consulship. It requires hysteria to drag it away from the muteness of mere forces. Where are there opportunities to free oneself by a swift decision? WHAT IS AN 18TH BRUMAIRE OF THE EMOTIONS? WHAT IS A BONAPARTIST OF LOVE?

In France the century is such that in the years up to 1812 all energies of resolution have been used up, an "entrepreneurial," "occupatory" (proprietorially expansive) decade. It is succeeded by a further swamp of irresolutions (Ancien régime) and of "ostensible decisions" (Second Empire): attentism.

Love, Recognizable for Having the Beloved's Interests at Heart

In the presence of Emma Saskissjan, who sang Carmen, the award-winning conductor Dimitri Kitayenko replied to questions submitted by the Western European correspondent:

Our "Carmen Interpretation" is the fruit of a close creative cooperation with the director F. The work's musical and dramatic form was explored not just with his support, but with the support of the entire collective. In a manner of speaking, we fell back on the groundwork performed by numerous artistic collectives that have grappled with *Carmen*'s form in the past, etc.

According to the director, it is an emotional odyssey, a switching of love objects. Micaela loves José, José loves Carmen, Carmen loves Escamillo, Escamillo loves no one but himself. This sequence would logically lead to a "fatal" series of events, i.e., the deaths of the protagonists.

Why Escamillo's death? Or Micaela's?
—Escamillo is killed by the bull, Micaela ends up in her village as a kind of zombie.
—But now the collective of the Moscow Stanislawsky-Nemirovich-Danchenko Musical Theater has developed a counterconcept?
—That's right. And the director F. picked up on this concept and implemented it with our collective assistance.
—And the premise is?
—The premise is that Escamillo loves Carmen. Trying to impress her, he is killed in the bullfight. Meanwhile, as we know, Carmen does *not* love José (at least in the end). But José doesn't love Carmen either. Micaela, left over from a previous village marital project, doesn't love Don José. None of this provides any grounds for dramatic developments. It's possible for the three to reach an agreement.

—And that's a better version?

—We worked it out that way.

—Meaning that you act out all the characters' various errors, poker-faced?

—That's the message of the opera. It's about those sorts of delusions. The characters in the opera act like amateurs as far as the ideal of love is concerned. They don't understand a thing about it.

—Or they aren't in love.

—That's probably it. Otherwise they'd consider the interests of the beloved.

—Isn't that what Micaela does the whole time?

—Yes, but so amateurishly. If she were in love, she'd find ways and means. Human beings are capable of learning.

—Is that the opera's message?

—In our interpretation.

—Isn't the plot a bit over-elaborate for that?

—That's our view. Each of these errors could be cleared up *quickly*.

—The opera would end up being shorter?

—Yes. Then more contemporary pieces could be included in the repertoire.

The Great Welaschka

Of lowly rank—
highly gifted.

The soprano Hanni Welaschka was far better known, more disciplined and thus more diligent than her long-time lover David F.; she even seemed more persevering and inspired in her pleasures, in applying art and pride to her style, life, etc.

All the same, she was unable to improve on her initial standing; indeed, her position with respect to David, already severely diminished in the first moments of infatuation, slipped several notches. She stood no chance of competing with David's long-standing friend and colleague. She always saw the two friends' broad backs in front of her. They went on ahead, and she, the star, was expected to follow.

Seeing this convoy, the journalists in the ballroom regarded her, the celebrity, as a kind of lamp meant to illuminate the two friends' backs. Yes, people would say, that's the long-time lover of the famous Welaschka, and next to him is his colleague and friend. They said nothing about her, because it seemed to go without saying that she was Welaschka. But it didn't go without saying; she had to earn it all over again every day.

The two men's friendship, which Welaschka reinforced when she pleasured one of them at night in the starlight, made her remain a sort of thing: a public thing while she worked, and a private thing while she facilitated pleasure, whatever that meant for her as a genuine life-thing.

Moment of Decision

"Give Father your consent, and tomorrow he shall be your husband ..." But of her, the matchmaking father says: "Believe me, she's as true as she is beautiful ..." The woman has been sold, indeed recognized, which is more than mere acquisition. Does Wagner have a sense of humor?

—Would you jump in after me to save me?
—Jump where?
—Into the cold water of a harbor on a Nordic fjord?
—To save you?

—Yes.

—Is that the only option?

—Tell me honestly. It'll mean nothing for our relationship otherwise.

—I'd jump in after you.

—You're lying!

She realized that he tended to lie when he saw no other way to make her be quiet. They walked a few steps farther.

—You don't have to jump, I'm just asking. After all, I'm not the Flying Dutchman, she says, but what if I were?

—Then I'd jump in after you to save you.

—I don't believe you.

—After all, replied Emil Mölders, you aren't the Flying Dutchman.

His fiancée, accompanying him out of the opera house into the Munich night, was, being a woman, certainly not the Flying Dutchman, who, misinterpreting from afar the conversation between the hunter and Senta, believes his betrothed to be unfaithful and plunges into the harbor. Senta plunges after him. Both rise up into the heavens.

The story, which moved me, said Hilde, holds no joyful prospects whatsoever. How could I rise up with you for redemptive reasons from the filthy Munkmarsch harbor water, to take an example we're both familiar with, where we can't even drown at low tide because it's too shallow, how could we rise up toward the solid land of heaven, when we both know that what's up there is the stratosphere, then the Van Allen Belt and the empty air of outer space, with no dwelling place whatsoever?

—You can't say AIR OF OUTER SPACE, Emil replied.

Why do I get agitated, persisted Hilde, when faced with grand, absurd emotions, though I stay cool when the questions are realistic, for instance whether I should buy salami to redeem you from your evening hunger? Does that mean there's no time and place for grand emotions?

Clearly that's what art is trying to tell us, replied Emil, who wanted to drop in for a nightcap at Leopold. He needed to get a taxi, but the argument was getting in the way. Just a moment! said Hilde. You can't fob me off like that. Inwardly she lingered over the image of Senta standing motionless, her gaze fixed on the apparition of the ghostly man stepping through the door of the merchant's house, but now the engaged couple had to hurry to the taxi stand to head straight for Leopold. There they'd meet people Hilde had no desire to see because they jarred with the lingering mood of the opera, the spectral sailors, and the Nordic trading depot.

But next to them and ahead of them other operagoers were hurrying to catch taxis, and so for objective reasons the two had to move quickly to nab one for themselves. This struck Hilde as nonsensical.

Why, she asked, must we go to the opera if we have to be in such a hurry afterward; to her the opera seemed an ideal exercise in TAKING EMOTIONAL TEMPI MORE SLOWLY. What I mean, she said, is that art wants to tell us something. Surely it doesn't just mean that we should constantly be seeing ghosts. In this case, God's vengeance strikes me as too long-term, if anything. The fact that this Dutchman laughed at the wrong moment some time thirty years after Christ's birth (or around Christ's death) needn't condemn him to a journey lasting into the twentieth century. God is tenacious, but not persnickety. The story, Emil replied, is set in 1810, not in the twentieth century. That's still too long, Hilde retorted. She found Emil's response superficial. Please focus on my question, she said. I'm asking: What is art trying to tell us, considering that for several hours while watching this opera I was able to accommodate or set in motion large-scale emotions, but now I can't. At the same time, God's vengeance is too long. They had reached the taxi stand. There were no more taxis. What kind? asked Emil. What? said Hilde. What kind of large-scale emotions, what direction would yours take? Emil hadn't been completely unmoved either; he was asking out of kindness. She was unable to reply.

The conversation left her disappointed. Opening a taxi door at last, she had to decide at that moment whether to see Emil as superficial (unmindful of her, and with a hectic disregard of his own emotions too) or whether she might "have some rudimentary basis" to go on living with him. Then she jumped after him into the car.

You can't treat us like that, she thought. It took her several days to realize what it meant that she'd followed Emil without a word, though she'd actually wanted to talk about what art was trying to tell them. She had calculated (looking at her watch) that it took seventeen minutes for Senta and the Dutchman to come to an understanding about the first glance they exchanged. Hilde, lacking artistic training, assumed that she herself would have taken thirty minutes to correctly interpret even one of Emil's harried looks or the movement of his hand to the taxi door. It was unfair, how little time there was for all the movements she performed each day.

And so that evening she began to doubt whether art had anything to say to them, vacillating in her assessment only because he was so set on going to Leopold, which in turn was only because he'd promised to show up there. When they walked into Leopold, her eyes lingered on no one. For their friends it went without saying that they'd appear as promised. Have a seat, Emil, one of them said. Hilde felt like bursting into tears.

"Taking emotional tempi more slowly."

The Death of Wieland Wagner

> *The pounding of a jackhammer either destroys you or toughens you up*
> *Gertrud Wagner*

The women, Gertrud Wagner and her daughters, had been given a room in the clinic. But they all moved into the dying man's room. They touched him, listened to his breath. Around 10 p.m. the nurse gave him an injection to ease his death struggle. The GREAT MAN's breath rattled, he made soft noises.

A telephone stood on the nightstand. A call from his mistress. Having finished singing a premiere in Vienna, she was trying to reach the man she didn't know was dying. At most she sensed danger. He can't come to the phone, replied Gertrud, her rival.

She hung up. How could he have phoned, his breath rattling in his throat? She barricaded the dying man against all disturbances.

A doctor came and took his pulse. The man died around 1 a.m. The four women, Gertrud and her daughters, felt that just before dying his features had "lit up." They saw dawn breaking outside. Rain was pouring down. But as the hours passed the light grew grayer, then brighter.

Around 7 a.m., one of the children looked out the window of the death room and saw the mistress drive up in a car. She walked into the room and started screaming. The children led her out into the hall. An agreement was reached: the family would remain in the dead man's room until 9 a.m., then vacate it for the mistress so that she could take her leave as well. In barbaric times, the dead man would have been cut apart so that each of the hostile parties would have a piece to mourn, cart away and burn. But now, under the dictatorship of civilization, of day dawning in the clinic, the enemies took shifts, and by 11 a.m. the dead man was moved onto a gurney and transported back to his hometown.

The conflict between the widows—legitimate and illegitimate, both beloved (the dead man would have liked to be consistent, and live with both women at once)—was waged afterward in the mass media. Neither of them came out victorious; the wife was ruthlessly disinherited by her brother-in-law and the mistress was not entitled to any concrete claims. The "laughing" third party easily disinherited the wife—the media presence of the mistress, "the real wife" (Brünnhilde, so to speak), undercut the naïve spouse obsessed with sheer legitimacy (Gudrun). And so the children and the wife could claim the dying man's final blessing (or breath), momentary possession of the corpse, control over the funeral, but nothing else. The GREAT MAN himself was disinherited and thrust into temporary oblivion by the banal routines of a mediocre third party.

NORMA, an Agglomeration of Magnanimity

Words, get up and follow me!
… onward, there's no end ahead.
Ingeborg Bachmann

1 Theme

In a world of warriors (the Romans and Gauls have the same war gods) a priestess known for her chastity has instituted a reform introducing lost matriarchal rites ascribed to the moon goddess. Put simply: it's all about peace.

But this revolutionary woman is not a "new type of human being," nor is she chaste; she has an erotic secret (revealed in circumspect nineteenth-century spirit). Just before a (possible) reconciliation can take place, a tragic chain of events occurs. To prevent an annihilating massacre, Norma sacrifices herself. This wins back Pollione's admiration, which he expresses by offering up his own life.

2 Anna Viebrock's Set Design

The set designer Anna Viebrock has given the stage the staggered depth of a church nave, like a Huguenot temple. In front of the grille that demarcates the foreground of the stage, as though the sanctum were on the side of the audience, stands the heroine: Norma. Behind her the devout. The druidess turns her back on them. Why doesn't she look in their direction, why doesn't she coerce them with her eyes, like an animal tamer? Does she trust them? She has no reason to. She is shattering religious assumptions about war, military decrees, the cruelty of the gods. Prophets like her have been murdered since time immemorial.

It's important to Norma to drag these believers onward. As though from the depths of a laterna magica's machinery, as she sings the aria CASTA DIVA the moonlight shines through the back windows of the stage, in support of the priestess. Light of the olden days, working only in the absence of the sun.*

We are told of a battle between the matriarchy and the patriarchy, Anna Viebrock notes, long before the brothers conspired to kill the father and before the fratricidal struggle. But none of this, the set designer adds, unfolded fully so as to be brought to an end. Natural catastrophes intervened (cometary impacts, earthquakes, floods, the plague). People fled. In this exodus the homicidal group scattered, producing a new beginning that could cope with hybridity. Hybrids survived. And so it is a never-ending struggle.

Who is speaking? Who can say "I"? The *I* seldom can. If it holds still, it can hear echoes speaking. Only the echoes themselves know how they fit together. The GREAT DISPERSAL listens. That is how Heiner Müller described it. Whoever can read this dispersal hears something say "I," polyglot, in chorus. And dreams, hope? They aren't listening.

—And you express that in the set design?

—Yes, that is my means of expression.

3 A Triumph of Friendship

The two wise women who love the same man—as they have just learned—express confusion.

----

* In the epochs of human history, the solar races are preceded by the age of lunar humanity. However, according to Rudolf Steiner, the most advanced elements of the previous epoch may be intellectually superior to the undeveloped elements of the more developed epoch. In this sense, *Norma* is the heroic, intelligent form of regression, the indispensable REAR GUARD OF PROGRESS (Heiner Müller). The Romans, up to Constantine, are sun warriors.

I loved him ... but my heart
feels nothing now but friendship

Adalgisa means her friendship with the druidess Norma, whom the Roman has just abandoned for her sake.

The only recourse is for the friend to speak to the malefactor in public. Adalgisa sets out for the Romans' camp.

She explains to the commander that his love for her, Adalgisa, is a mistake. How much finer, greater is Norma's character! How could he spurn such a human treasure, destroying it in the process?

The commander, recalling many a delightful hour with Adalgisa (yes, he's impressed by her splendid rhetorical performance, while sexually aroused by the thought of what might follow), remains uninterested in Norma. She is tiresome to him, with the seriousness of her emotions. He refuses to make any concessions. As though a man's romantic desire could be aroused by a woman's greater *virtue*!

Traitorous Roman! Adalgisa, doubtless still in love with him, carried away by fellowship with her friend, transported by the passionate élan of friendship, steals back along dark paths to the camp of the Gauls. Puts herself at the priests' disposal. She consecrates herself to death.

4 Verdun, the Great Slave Market

Yes, she weeps / What hope has she?
Her plea has been dismissed!
Norma, Act 2, final chorus

Shortly before his death Heiner Müller was invited by the Verdun municipal theater to visit that corner of what was once Gaul; he was to stage one of his plays there the following year and begin by acquainting himself with the location.* Having visited one of the city's military cemeteries, and having been criticized for a public remark he made regarding his impressions, he had a falling-out with the city government, was disinvited, and departed.

In the fluvial landscape of Verdun, Müller jotted down on a beer coaster, a handful of clay remains self-identical over the course of 3,000 years. When this soil is churned up by artillery, when its surface is worked over by agriculture or the construction of towns and highways, the alteration in the molecules, as measured against the borders of Europe, is insignificant.

From the years 782 to 804 A.D. this was the largest market for slaves. A slave, taken captive in war, carted in from the lands of the Germans, can achieve happiness if the latifundium that purchases him is administered in a spirit of kindness, and if he can find a compatible woman slave. A female descendent, assuming things begin and progress felicitously, may have the chance to enchant a Frankish warrior and join the ruling class herself.

From the perspective of the seventh century's CONFEDERATED PROMISES OF HAPPINESS, it is a fluke that the military staffs of 1916 chose these hills and plains—in a zone of the earth now defined as a fortress—to implement their project of BLOODLETTING. Museums, graves, memorial plaques commemorate it. How quickly does a landscape scar over?

Interview with Heiner Müller in Verdun:

—You described the sanctums of the dead, the monuments and chapels of Verdun's cemeteries as "kitschy": as battle kitsch.
—At any rate they don't convey the way people were firing at each other here back in 1916.
—What distinguishes slaves from soldiers in the trenches, pinned down amidst the artillery barrage by their orders?

---

* At that time the stoic man, aware of his terminal illness, gladly took on commissions scheduled for the distant future.

—A lot. Slaves can hope for good treatment.

—The soldiers in the trenches have no hope?

—Not really. Because even if they go home, nothing is adequate to the experience of being exposed to the mortar barrage. All they can do with the memory is extinguish it.

—How is a slave defined?

—As a person or a unit of working power who is someone else's property.

—Whose property are the soldiers of 1916? The wounded men? The shattered men?

—On the German side, the property of the Reich. On the French side, the property of the Republic.

—In that sense they're slaves too?

—No. They possess a will of their own, which desires to leave this battlefield at all costs. A slave had no right to this will.

—Not by law, or not in reality?

—I can't put myself in the position of a slave from 602 A.D.

—And one of those suits of *character armor* from 1916, lying here outside Verdun?

—Not that either.

5 Battle on the Border of the "I"

> *The heart is the final dimension*
> *of intelligence.*
> Marcel Proust (on Baron Charlus)

Maestro Reynaldo Hahn was an outstanding conversationalist. "The heart pulls a fast one on the intellect." Phrases like these drift through Hahn's mind all morning, yet he finds no opportunity to slip the epigram into one of the day's many chats. Among Marcel Proust's closest friends, Reynaldo Hahn was the only one suited to perform a public role. He was a critic for *Le Figaro* and director of the Théâtre de Casino in Cannes. He survived Proust and carried on the conversational tradition of their clique.

After the liberation of Paris in 1944, he was regarded as politically untainted, and was made director of the Paris Opera in 1945. Sixteen premieres had to be lined up. Possibilities included Massenet (*Werther*), Cherubini (*Medea*), Saint-Saëns, Berlioz (*Les Troyens*), Bellini (*Norma*). An attractive young director thought it appropriate to costume the Gaulish heroine Norma as Jeanne d'Arc, producing an opera of revolution. Magnanimously Hahn indulged him in this fit of bad taste.

—You are politically independent, Monsieur Director.

—Politically independent.

—And you are a homosexual?

—Whatever that means. It doesn't mean I'm a leper.

—And now, in your production of Norma, you advocate passionately for the cause of women?

—For a woman victim.

—The production inspires a deep appreciation of these Gaulish women.

—That's why we chose this opera, which is so effective on stage. Norma appears in the costume of the Maid of Orleans.

—You aren't appalled by the bad taste?

—It's a bit too direct. But you can safely assume that homoerotic men always hold women in veneration.

—Now back to the opera. While Norma is dying you have people carry banners to the front of the stage (preparations are already being made during the duet between Norma and Pollione), displaying words that the French language gives a feminine gender: *la bataille, la nation, la guerre.* Are you making fun of the fact that the warlike virtues are supposed to be feminine?

—Am I warlike?

—What is warlike?

—Whatever makes us forget the war between the sexes.

—So you mean war is superficial?
—It's dangerous enough.

Hahn (center) at the front, Verdun, 1916.

Baron Charlus, still part of the clan in 1916, found his heart (which ruled his keen intellect like a tyrant) drawn to the young soldiers who loitered about the Gare Montparnasse in the second year of the war. They had to be warlike ne'er-do-wells, effigies of battle's violence. The high-ranking nobleman desired them to subjugate him in a pissoir. He wanted to be their victim; taking on the likeness of the enemies who were storming France in 1916, he approached them as a Prussian matron (something he didn't resemble in the slightest), as "Madame Boche." The soldiers, never once on a level with his intellect, seeking an adventure with a young female traveler or a prostitute before their furlough ended, mocked this monstrous-seeming holder of a heart. They believed (erroneously) that war was simply a menacing burden, not an aggregate state of sexuality.

At the premiere of *Norma* at the Palais Garnier, there was a certain danger that the corpulent singer of the title role, performing in the additional accoutrements of a freedom fighter, might seem ridiculous when she momentarily embraced the enemy general in the last act. The audience knew her as Brünnhilde. Now, as a Celtic defector, she would lead her beloved foe to the sacrifice. In the event of an utter fiasco, Reynaldo Hahn had a substitute play at the ready: GOTT MIT UNS, a drama (from 1928) by René Berton. During World War I, French soldiers seize a bunker previously defended by the Germans. Just as the French soldiers advance into the bunker, a German bomb hit buries the entrance. A single German soldier, Hermann, has been left behind. Knowing that a time bomb is hidden here, he is trying to dig his way out of the ill-fated hole. As a patriot, he refuses to tell the intruders, his foes, the location of the bomb. The French captain, in civilian life a philosophy professor, just like Hermann, persuades him to defuse the bomb. In the meantime, a French sapper unit has dug its way through the blocked entrance to the bunker. Hermann is the first to run outside. He is struck by a German bullet. His face obliterated, he goes back into the bunker, cries "*Gott mit uns*" and dies.

Reynaldo Hahn wanted to accompany these scenes with melodies from Bellini's opera, which was feasible if the dialogue and singing were left out. But due to the elated mood of the audience in summer 1945, the premiere of *Norma* (and the rest of the repertoire) was a great success. There was no need for the substitute play.

6 Enigmatic Gaul

Love emerging from slavery and conquest. The Franks, marching into the country, were fascinated not by the Roman women, nor by the genteel wives of the Gauls who administered the rural estates, but by those estates' slaves. The conquerors and the slave women had something in common: with their bond, a new life began.*

Only later did the new couples expropriate the old owners. Now property consorted with intimacy.†

Who was to be subjugated? The warrior? The slave? That was impossible to straighten out. But it's said that the NEW BONDS described here are what makes the difference between France and a barbarian land.

7 Einar Schleef's Production at the Volksbühne on Rosa-Luxemburg-Platz

Druids, Gaulish warriors, Romans (in identical costumes: the coats of Wehrmacht soldiers returning from war captivity). The women: Norma, Adalgisa, Clotilde (in the garb of the knights from *Parsifal* and *Lohengrin*, i.e., dazzling white and silver suits of armor). The choruses act as combat units. They fight "spectral skirmishes." At times they gather around tables where they imbibe poison or blood.

TAGESZEITUNG: Herr Schleef, you're accused of massacring Bellini. You've cut the music down to six choruses and six duets. You undermine the dramatic tension by summarizing the plot at the

---

* They occupied broad swathes of Gaul. They were viewed as conquerors. They did not have better weapons or better reasons to occupy the country than the inhabitants of Gaul, the old families. It was merely that they met with no resistance. Just one year later, or three years earlier, the coup would have failed.

† This, Jules Michelet writes, is how feudalism arose ("I serve you because you serve me"), the foundation for the only basic form of love invented in Europe.

beginning in the past perfect tense. What is more, you expand Bellini's great dramatic arc with a sequence of interruptions, blurring the boundary between interpolation and original by superimposing Bellini's music.

SCHLEEF: The critics crucified me for it.

TAGESZEITUNG: You completely omitted the scene in which Norma tries to kill her two children, replacing it with a scene inserted from Cherubini's *Medea*. Why?

SCHLEEF: Medea has a compelling reason to kill her children. She is indomitable. She wants to punish the traitor Jason, her husband. She wants to obliterate her previous life. All exactly as in Bellini's Norma, except that the logical action is actually taken. "Wrong life cannot be lived rightly."

TAGESZEITUNG: Norma hesitates.

SCHLEEF: With good reason. She is the more radical of the two. She discards the direct means of emotional retribution. She leaves the children out of it. That's why I left out the scene. Medea commits the murder. Norma leaves it out.

TAGESZEITUNG: But you don't show that.

SCHLEEF: How can you stage something that doesn't take place?

TAGESZEITUNG: Norma approaches the children with a drawn dagger (or, in Stuttgart, a revolver), hesitates, and then retreats.

SCHLEEF: How silly.

TAGESZEITUNG: But it isn't a game.

SCHLEEF: Certainly not. But the expression "bloody serious" is just as wrong-headed.

TAGESZEITUNG: Thus the death by fire?

SCHLEEF: Like the death of the Valkyrie in Act 3 of *Götterdämmerung*.

TAGESZEITUNG: But you don't show any fire.

SCHLEEF (angrily): I don't want to burn any witches.

TAGESZEITUNG: Why are Brünnhilde and Norma witches?

SCHLEEF: That's just it, there aren't any witches.

TAGESZEITUNG: But in operas there are women who die by fire. In Halévy's *La Juive* the heroine dies in a cauldron of boiling oil.

SCHLEEF: Not in my production.

TAGESZEITUNG: Going by the principle of the phoenix from the ashes?

SCHLEEF (even angrier, face red): I don't do principles. It's practicality.

TAGESZEITUNG: Is it practical for the theater when you leave out the exciting end?

SCHLEEF: What's exciting about a woman's immolation?

TAGESZEITUNG: That's the ending Bellini envisages.

SCHLEEF: So much the worse.

TAGESZEITUNG: But my dear Herr Schleef, you're the one who claims to be guided by the original text.

SCHLEEF: Our hearts must burn.

TAGESZEITUNG: Instead of Norma?

SCHLEEF: Exactly.

A German Philosopher in Persia

1

They're driving across the barren mountains, hour after hour. From a lecture hall in Tehran to an auditorium in the south. A practicing Shiite, a doctoral student, familiar with western works. She is the philosopher's chauffeur.

Once, at the Tehran Opera, she'd seen a production of a western music drama. She mentions a dialogue between a priestess and another, lower-ranking priestess in a classic land of the west. He's unfamiliar with the scene. She tries to explain it to him.

The special thing about such a journey is its duration. A journey through a rocky desert with majestic outcroppings also made of rock. You can't describe this terrain as mountains and valleys. It's an utterly alien world. What takes place between the philosopher and the driver can't be called a dialogue. It's a juxtaposition of different conceptions. The driver, evidently a religious believer, has special standards for practical earthly behavior: STANDARDS SHE DOESN'T WANT TO DISCUSS.

This philosopher, the doctoral student well knows, is famous for holding that there are no questions regarding practical earthly behavior that can't be put up for discussion. However far-fetched a stranger's utterance, there must be some procedure enabling exchange, barter. Otherwise one could only communicate via money and force.

After two hours in a swaying automobile, two people with a four hours' drive still ahead of them are no longer strangers.

2

Two priestesses of the moon goddess who controls Gaul's fate, both pledged to chastity, are seduced in succession and in great secrecy by a powerful Roman. The younger victim of seduction (but how can she be the victim of seduction, when she is the one who loves him) seeks counsel from the senior druidess, Norma. Can there be counsel in questions of intimacy? Can there be counsel among rivals?

As noted, the philosopher was unfamiliar with the scene. Evidently the issue was religious transgression (chastity/secret concubinage), combined with a conflict between nationalities (Gaulish patriots/Romans), linked to a complex of questions relating to romantic betrayal (vows of erotic faithfulness, the impossibility of honoring such things as contracts in the realm of the libido). One finds discussions of the matter in critical theory and in the work of Sigmund Freud, as well as relevant examples in life experience and in the western literary tradition (*Anna Karenina, Madame Bovary, In Search of Lost Time*). As the philosopher understands it, the Roman has abandoned his former lover, with whom he has two children, for a younger and more attractive woman.

The theocratic regime is unfamiliar with the philosopher's works. Otherwise it never would have let him into the country. Thus the philosopher's right to hospitality is guaranteed only by the isolated faction that invited him. It turns out that part of his young chauffeur's soul leans toward orthodoxy, while part leans toward the reformers. But the soul is indivisible; so is the right to hospitality. This hospitality embraces his thoughts as well. She listens to him.*

3 *Killing Religion by Kindness?*

The doctoral student is hardly timid. Not for a moment does the professor feel it would be possible to embroil her in compromises. That impresses him.

What is faith? An ATTITUDE WITH NO ROOM FOR NEGO-TIATION. Difficult terrain for the man of the Enlightenment. It must continue to be possible to dissolve any hermetic position in the world by asking nagging questions. Someday, somewhere, a planet-spanning river of understanding must emerge, making thoughts as useful as commodities. Are thoughts transmitted through friendliness? Must religious people fear this friendliness because it can induce them to make compromises? Goodness is not friendly. There's a certain severity in the thought that understanding follows a law.

---

* Given a position of non-secular religiosity ("serious must remain serious"), the case of *Norma* will undergo a different analysis than from a stance of discursive competence ("people must not be victimized").

Outside, as before, rocky desert. The philosopher has trouble imagining all the times civilization here has been destroyed by conquering peoples, raiding tribes, before that the Mongols. What would a Roman envoy from Crassus or one of the barracks emperors recognize as familiar in the highlands of Persia? The philosopher's interlocutor, taking pains to buffer the bumps in the road, attempts to explain to him—he's long since grasped the thrust of her argument—the extent to which friendly conversations destroy the SERIOUSNESS OF RELIGION.

More like Fire Gods

The fecklessness of the Roman who seduced Norma is only the surface, as it turns out. The praetor spontaneously embraces a fiery death with Norma. Love must burn.

On this point, it struck the European philosopher, his chauffeur was not actually a Shiite, but a disciple of the Zoroastrian death by fire.

Love must burn, repeated the driver, or it is not love. The same is true of every state of emotion in history or current reality.

To the philosopher it sounded as though his Eastern traveling companion was explaining the concept of ALIENATION. "To escape from alienation, one must return along the same path that led into alienation." He is agnostic, but not about the assumptions on which the concept of the polity is based. As described by Jules Michelet, the idea of the polity arose in France when conquering Franks formed bonds with Roman slave women; the idea arose in ardent hearts and was later capable of mollifying public violence.

Darkness descended. The headlights lanced out at the gravel road.

It turns out that both priestesses are in love with the same man. The one who comes to the supreme druidess for counsel has a taboo relationship. Flying in the face of all psychology, says the Persian driver, the two women, one of them betrayed, the other affirmed, form an *understanding* that can be explained only by the principle of FRIENDSHIP. In this opera's exuberance of feeling, the Persian explains, the rival, Adalgisa, disavows her love. Out of friendship to Norma, she plans to head at once to the Roman camp to praise the worthiness of Norma's character to her Roman lover. Thus, COMMUNICATION must supply the means to fetch the straying lover back into the druidess's secret love nest in the sacred woods of Gaul.

The philosopher, jostled about in the automobile, asks: Will that work out, judging from life experience? What does the rival praise? Norma's worthiness of character? What the seducer has lost? The moonlight? The memory of some detail? We don't know, the Persian doctoral student explains, how Norma's rival expressed herself in this public speech. She is standing in front of a Roman assembly and a mortified praetor.

The philosopher tries to imagine the unfamiliar situation. He senses that his Persian traveling companion isn't asking him about romantic questions, but rather about central aspects of his theory of communication.

Can a Romantic Relationship Be a Capital Crime?

Following the failure of her speech to the Roman praetor, Adalgisa embraces the absolute obligation of friendship and surrenders to the priests in the sacred woods, willing to face execution. Word comes that a Roman raiding party, including the praetor, has been captured by Gaulish guards in an attempt to free the foolish Adalgisa.

If I've understood the plot of Bellini's opera correctly, the philosopher went on, it's negotiated against the background of a progressively decaying religious principle (in the nineteenth century, Gaulish beliefs no longer hold) and on the basis of a skeptical phase of national pride (France would never subjugate itself to Prussia, but would submit to the more universal Rome without hesitation, as in the Treaties of Rome); at the same time, it's about the triumph of spontaneity in love. It's not impossible for passionate skin contact and obsession to turn spontaneously into friendship.

That wasn't how the Shiite interpreted the story. Had she misunderstood the philosopher? Friendship is not divided by passion; she rejoined; passion is not divided by guilt.

The Annihilation of Emotion

Love strikes down religious precepts. Religion strikes back, compelling martyrdom.* The Persian doctoral student at the wheel speaks of a decadent tendency in western literature. The philosopher tries to qualify this: In the genre of Italian opera. No, the doctoral student insists, the cynical offsetting of all values, making them annihilate one another, that's western fundamentalism. Nothing works without barter. Barter is obligatory. But religion doesn't barter.

Then how can we imagine the solution of a conflict? asks the philosopher. The epochs of religiosity, and hopefully national-

---

* There is a long chain of confusion; it begins in Norma's heart, when she feels hurt, and leads to the Gauls' massacre of the Romans, who will in turn avenge the Gauls' revolt.

ism as well, were being phased out, and a fundamental principle of differentiation would prevail, allowing new value systems to form.

The chauffeur replied that she didn't believe that. On what basis didn't she believe it? The Persian was silent, dumbfounded. On no basis but what I believe. It was absurd, she went on, to fall back on some third thing to affirm one's own belief. Enlightenment consisted of using one's belief without anyone else's guidance. Otherwise belief would be non-autonomous. "Autonomous belief" struck the philosopher as an interesting inversion. The Persian had told him that Norma's longtime love had produced two children. Despite her rage, Norma found herself unable to kill them (as Medea had). Here, suggested the philosopher, Bellini departed from traditional religion. One emotion hesitates to annihilate another.

5 Now I Lay Me Down to Sleep

Sheltered in the bone structure of the skull: the brain, restlessly at work. Surrounding the vulnerable human body, already rattled about for six hours in the automobile: a solid metal shell cutting it off from the heat of the country. The country's hospitality is invisible, a precarious protection.

The philosopher is sleepy. How can one uphold, for the seven hours from Tehran to Isfahan, the fundamental assumption that all things in the human interior and the global exterior are open to peace negotiations, i.e., to discussion? At some point, at nightfall, the will to fight, source of the Enlightenment, grows weary. Within a radius of 4,000 miles around Tehran we find one-third of the world's problems, two-thirds of its crude oil, half of its wealth, two-thirds of its poverty. At any time the U.S.A. can cause chaos in this tableau of events across which Persia gazes from the north. That would be devastating for the next generation. The philosopher is troubled. Does secularization only have a chance when nations grow weary? Or do the patient reactions of the Shiite at the wheel show that there is a second kind of secularization, not devised by corruptible German princes, not echoing the expropriation of the priests in France in 1791, but developed from the seriousness of the ideal that prevails across the globe and blows through all events as the WIND OF HISTORY?

In the moment of weariness, the imagination falls to pieces. It is time to contemplate the individual fragments.

How could the philosopher, in his jostled state, explain to the doctoral student the concept of seriousness as a common currency, the fragment of Walter Benjamin's "Capitalism as Religion," a mere eight pages long? It contains the seeds of a new secularization. At the same time, it respects the fact that religion can in no way be influenced by rhetoric. But in any case rhetoric is not the philosopher's tool. What does communication mean? Surely not just speech.

Figaro's Loyalty

We know that Figaro, protagonist of the hit play *The Mad Day* by Beaumarchais and the Mozart opera named after him, was not of noble blood, nor was the Countess. Evidently the two had been childhood sweethearts before she married the count.

Every morning thereafter, Figaro caressed this young woman's hair, made up her face for the day. He was continually drawn to her. He gave her advice, as we know, on how to preserve her marriage. He did not exploit his intimate proximity to her hair and her ear, her side and her back for intrigues. The tenderness of his hands and his straying thoughts stayed restrained (unlike the incest taboo, but resembling a loyalty taboo, something long-familiar yet novel, rarely defined in literature: Thou shalt not betray the interests of the one you love). The relationship which the Count and Countess arranged between Figaro and Susanna, which seems so perfect in the finale of Mozart's opera, did not survive the turmoil of the 1789 revolution. Susanna began a career as a secretary for the Committee of Public Safety. The Count and Countess were held in a Paris prison. Figaro was now the head of a revolutionary tribunal. The Count and Countess came before him as defendants. Figaro could easily have condemned his rival, the Count, to be executed, thus gaining power over the Countess. He did nothing of the sort. Soon afterward the Count and Countess escaped through the Ardennes and moved into a private house on the far side of the Rhine in Koblenz, where a large colony of emigrés lurked, waiting for some shift in current events.

A short while later Figaro, now an influential, high-powered man, followed his former masters. In Koblenz he was much sought after as a counselor, hairdresser, and costume designer. Even in German circles. And so, as a "servant" or as a "master," he supported the Count's household with his income. Soon the intimate emotion of the morning hours spent on the Countess's hair and face once again took tender form.

After the king's return (the upheaval of the Napoleonic wars was now over), the Count and Countess, no longer young, returned to the French estates that had been restored to them. They left Figaro behind. During the frequent regime changes, as his actions were not dictated by political advantage, he had often ended up on the wrong side, and so aristocratic circles now regarded him as a washout. Nor had he kept up with the fashions.

He went on working as a provincial hairdresser on the Rhine. He had learned German. He had three sisters, not mentioned in Mozart's opera. He had no descendants of his own, but his sisters had sixteen children. The family name, originally Spanish, was famous.

Additional Remarks by Dr. Boltzmann

From the perspective of evolutionary biology, Dr. Boltzmann informs us, Figaro's position in this sequence of true events initially seems to be a negative one. With his superior physical strength, even as a young man Figaro could have thrashed and scared off the Count as he wooed Susanna. That's what an animal would have done. Later, as the head of the revolutionary tribunal, he should have gone for the Count's jugular. He would have gained the Countess for himself, and thus the chance to have his own bevy of children.

But in fact, according to Dr. Boltzmann, Figaro's conduct, the principle of his actions, does have something going for it. He developed a novel terrain on which to exercise the force of tenderness and expand it in manifold ways (this terrain, an achievement of antiquity, had been lost by the eighteenth century). This innovation had the effect of a new heavenly body enhancing a constellation. New contradictions arose, but a greater number of old contradictions was cleared up. And it was not out of the question that such a position, that of a "lucky auxiliary star," might even result in children.

"Take the violinist on the sinking liner / The tone is painfully rich and mellow"

An unknown composition by Luigi Nono from 1966: seventy of the waiters who went down with the Titanic in 1912 came from neighboring villages in the Abruzzi. Not one of their fiancées, who had hoped that these men would return home and marry

---

"Take the violinist …": the title is taken from a poem by Ben Lerner.

them once they'd been paid their wages, ever found anyone else who would. The villages remained childless, and today stand desolate among the mountains. It was to these VOICELESS PEOPLE OF HISTORY that Nono dedicated his *Lament for Twelve Strings and Twelve Sopranos* in 1966. The grief is not so much for the waiters lost at the bottom of the sea as it is for the miserable fate of the women left behind, who were forbidden by strict local custom from seeking another husband in neighboring towns.

IV *Reality Challenges Theater for Top Billing*

Snow on a Copper Roof

The building houses a state opera. The art form this building serves has existed since 1607. More than four hundred years of opera. The opera impresario Schulz worked out that there are eighty thousand opera scores. He conjectured that, if they were all gathered together, they would form a single score, something like a CITY of music.

Commitment to a Colleague with a Sore Throat

In February 2013 the virulent lung infection that had been going around threw the program of one of Germany's leading opera houses into utter disorder. The singer playing the title role in *Rigoletto* at Munich's Bavarian State Opera lay miserably stricken on his hotel bed, his chest covered in hot packs. There was no way he could sing. By one o'clock that afternoon, the singer playing Falstaff at Milan's opera house had been ordered to get in a car. He set off over the Alps for the Bavarian capital. Just a quarter of an hour before the orchestra began its general rehearsal, he was being shown his place in the wings by assistants. There remained seven minutes for discussions with the principal conductor. The substitute baritone from Milan sang his part so proficiently and "with such tender strength" (opposite a Gilda who stood twenty yards away from him, who'd had to coordinate her movements with the dramaturge playing his part on stage, and whom he'd

never met) that—following his monologue to the servile court-
iers in the second act—the orchestra members drummed upon
their instruments, an honor rarely shown to someone performing at the opera house for the first time. Just twenty minutes after
the moving end of the opera, the singer, who could sing sixteen
different parts from Verdi's operas, was put in his car and driven
through the night back to Milan. The next morning at eleven
o'clock the same baritone appeared for the dress rehearsal of
Falstaff in the northern Italian capital.

The Iron Ring that Conquered the Cliff

When Schlingensief realized his life span was about to drastically
shorten, he focused his poetic eye on REDEMPTION. Twice he
found a particular way of expressing it. At the end of his *Parsifal*
at Bayreuth—at that time, he didn't yet know he had cancer—a
projection is seen (after the disintegration of his "resurrection
rabbit," *Wiedergeburtshase*): a gate leading to an upper heaven
from the film *Star Wars*. The image ultimately takes over the entire stage, but remains blurry.

The second version of his parting statement was more subtle.
In the final act of his Bavarian State Opera version of MEA CULPA,
he planned for Isolde's "Liebestod" to be sung. For the heroine,
he cast a singer of advanced age. Her vocal cords were worn out,
and in this state her throat made the "Liebestod" a devastating experience. Radio stations and media companies refused to broadcast the recording due to its poor quality, failing to recognize the
irrefutable beauty of the scene. In her singing, something of the
prospect of "love" remained. Which is not unlike how an elev-
enth-century shepherdess's capacity for devotion helped a young
knight to flee. The shepherdess sealed her bond with her beloved
by making him a present of a cheap iron ring. After the knight was

taken prisoner by his fiercest rival and incarcerated in a castle high on a cliff, he used the ring to grind a hole in the sandstone—with the image of the maiden so firmly impressed in his mind, the courage and patience for such tedious toil never failed him. When he was finally free, the knight arrived at a cliff overlooking an abyss, which set an objective limit to his flight. That the shepherdess's beloved could not be saved saddened the audience at Schlingensief's revue. To console them, the director, already goaded onward by cancer and drawing on his last theatrical reserves, sent in the almost voiceless singer. She hit every note and, through the force of Wagnerian "phantasmagoria in notes," made the audience forget the unhappy story of the shepherdess and her unrescuable knight—the spectators were too focused on the question of whether or not the singer would hold out (she did), and on the fact that even the ruins of a Wagnerian construction could still massage the ear with curious sincerity.

Reality Challenges Theater for Top Billing

Two suicides of party officials. Things are getting serious. Couples who have been together for twenty years separate. Although the district administration in Magdeburg is still officially "guiding" us, the regime is collapsing. The clergy and their sons have our city firmly in hand.

The people (were the city larger, one could say "the masses") go out in the evenings not to our "People's Theater," but to Saint Martin's Church. Our city has more than its share of churches, and for years, they have been in standby mode. But now, since the summer, the municipal church has been functioning as a gathering place; it has become the unofficial city center. Spies for the Ministry of State Security hardly dare show up anymore at these town meetings.

We in the People's Theater are having a hard time of it. The Magdeburg administrators have stopped depositing the money into the accounts our salaries are paid from. Four premieres are scheduled for December 1989. We don't expect much of an audience. I've just come from the artistic director; he's worried about the future of the 252 company employees. We are a three-pronged theater—opera, plays, ballet—an ornament of the Workers' and Farmers' Republic, quite luxurious for our small city.

We belong to the "social superstructure," which, as everyone knows, does not revolutionize as quickly as the base. The program launching the winter season was planned a year and a half ago, and signed off on by authorities who no longer answer our calls. It's hard to get our people to concentrate on the final rehearsals, which are necessary for each of the premieres—even if only a fifth of the seats in the large theater will be filled. They hang around with the others at the rallies, hold discussions. No one is rehearsing. I'm responsible for public relations at the theater, and I've debated suggestions for alternatives with the director: a surprise late addition in lieu of one of the planned premieres.

FREEDOM OPERA IN THREE ACTS. First act: Six clerics nail theses to the church door of our city, to music from NABUCCO by Verdi. Second act: Magdeburg forbids the production of the play. No one obeys. At the end of this act, the entire ensemble appears as the chorus, including accounting, canteen staff, cleaning crew, backstage, lighting. Third act: three box offices on the stage, lines of patrons. Finale with ballet interlude. We don't have a final draft of the ending yet. Yesterday we submitted the idea to the city council, still composed of old party officials. They listened. Those old salts have been through a lot. They responded: the people won't want freedom as an opera, but as reality. Our artistic director also finds the suggestion too flamboyant. We would be better off, he says, putting our efforts into the three planned premieres. The singers should sing "as well as they can."

A project for the coming year is developed: the quick & fresh-new-ideas concept. Plays to be worked out collectively: *Lard on Ration Cards* (with a contemporary twist) and *Stories of Good-for-Something* (with ironic accent) will add pep, says the artistic director. I'm responsible for public relations, and I don't believe they will.

All of this is displaced by a hustle to get at least the planned projects for December taken care of.

> *Evita, a Musical*
> *Czar and Carpenter*
> *The Gypsy Baron*
> *Christmas Tales*

At the time, the planning of the program had represented a compromise between the demands of the headquarters in Berlin and Magdeburg on the one hand, and our theater directors on the other. There had to be something emotionally consoling (the musical), something that humorously incorporated our brothers in the east (Czar Peter the Great in Lortzing's opera), as well as something we'd had down for 40 years and that our ensemble was accustomed to (the work by Johann Strauss, which could almost be described as an opera, if one were to stage it seriously). Our orchestra and singers could also have put on LA FORZA DEL DESTINO, from the repertory three years ago. That play would have better suited the SERIOUSNESS AND SPIRITUAL RE-VIVAL with which the pastors were now dragging the populace along behind them. Too little, too late.

Nevertheless, the ballet interlude in the second act of THE GYPSY BARON needs to be rehearsed. I have to jump in. In summer the choreographer had given us the slip by emigrating to the West through Hungary; she left behind a heap of slackers for a dance collective. The dancers with costumes from CARMEN don't yet form a proper group. They are new and have to practice.

I'm ashamed that we're not in tune with the times. How can our dance troupe find its place in the "hurtling movement of our days"? How do we "horn in"? Should we move to Saint Martin's Church with those parts of the ballet interlude that are more or less rehearsed (I suggest this), and perform it as an interpolation into the event taking place there, a discussion of the future of the Old Town? Our house dramaturge advises against it. The public mood is heating up. People hang on the lips of the preachers as though Luther's purge of Germany were at hand. You can't have twelve scantily clad ballerinas showing up and offering a "good vibe."

Now, amid all the turmoil, we need to show our practical side. Our lighting staff could install electrical wiring in the salvageable buildings of the Old Town (which have been rotting away for years). Our bookkeepers could help out in City Hall. An auction of costumes and props at the fish market. The dramaturgy department is prepared to offer life coaching and matchmaking ("West-marriages"). As soon as we knew the wall would come down, we saw before us a theatrical no-man's-land all the way to Braunschweig. "We can perform to our hearts' content," said the director, "as long as we keep the door to the future open." Time gets compressed. A day feels as long as a year.

Today, twenty-five years later, I would know what to do. I just saw Peter Konwitschny's stage adaptation of Bach's cantata 102, "Herr, deine Augen sehen nach dem Glauben!" at the Theater Chur. Konwitschny takes the texts of the cantata literally. A solitary believer sits in an interrogation cell and in his last hour must make a conscientious reckoning of his life; we hear extremist demands being made of him. Interrogation experts as we know them from the Ministry for State Security play the extremists. We could have cast our Florestan from FIDELIO as the believer. It would have made an indelible impression. We could have run this in all five major churches, every weekday, as the People's Theater's contribution. "Theater goes beyond reality."

What we didn't think about in all the tumult was that we had LOVE AND INTRIGUE up our sleeve. The play had been part of our repertory for 40 years. We could have borrowed selections from the piano reduction of Verdi's LUISA MILLER as musical accompaniment. I would have styled Ferdinand as a Western lawyer with experience in rescuing Eastern firms. Luise, a fifteen-year-old local girl, falls in love with the savior! I go back and forth as to whether we would have had to give the thing a tragic ending. Reality is one thing, the stage is another. In this case, since the times were all about "flourishing landscapes," theater might actually have been more real than REALITY, which had never experienced such a dazzling breakthrough in our city as it did in December 1989—but which, just three years later, had already deflated. With the delay inherent in the "cultural superstructure," we could have made something beautiful out of it on the stage. Instead of the socialist propaganda evening we had in repertory, "The Dignity of Humanity Is in Your Hands" (Schiller, sparsely attended)—LOVE AND INTRIGUE, the new version (Schiller, full house). It would have been perfect, had it occurred to us in time.

Sunday August 4, 2013, Elmau

A conductor is here. He is carrying a child, roughly a year old, on his arm. His second wife is an actress who works at the Burgtheater in Vienna. I made a film about this conductor almost twenty years ago when he performed Gluck's ALCESTE at the Berlin State Opera. His wife wants to see what he looked like in so much younger a state. I have to get a DVD.

Alceste, an opera of surging emotions. It deals with a home-comer's fate. The King of Thebes, Admetus, has been fatally injured in war. He will only survive, the gods say, if someone else sacrifices themselves for him. Only his wife Alceste, who loves him, is prepared to do so. Admetus later accuses his wife of high-handedness; she cannot enter the kingdom of the dead without her husband's consent (states an earthly law). As they love each other, they both choose death.

Is there a comparable level of emotionality about any act of love from the end of the Second World War? Bernd Alois Zimmermann's music contains passages that point back to the war's end in 1945. One can be sure that there were examples of self-sacrifices in the reality of April 30, 1945: a Jewish secret agent goes far behind German lines to find his siblings, who had been sent on a death march from a concentration camp. He dies. A newlywed woman takes horses from her parents' country estate to her husband's trapped garrison so that they can escape together.

In addition to the stories in which one person sacrifices themselves for another, there is also the emotion of LIBERATION: those condemned to death, imprisoned or worn down suddenly find themselves liberated, or liberate themselves. That has not been set to music. But it forms a part of that day. The "dark God of pain" still reigns. So I imagine some funeral music.

Night of Decisions

In honor of the German Federal Chancellor Schmidt, an after-dinner performance of an operetta by Sullivan in the rose garden of the White House had been prepared. Sitting in armchairs that had been moved to the garden, the guests and their wives, the President, a few senators, and some foundation presidents sat facing the small orchestra and the singers. The space was tight. Thanks to the midsummer twilight, the light faded very slowly. Many of the event's visitors wished there could be a clear decision between the remaining sunlight and electric light.

Outside of this tiny venue where the ruling circle was spending the evening, dramatic events were taking place at the same time.

In New York there was an electricity blackout. In the skyscrapers the lights went out by the millions. People were trapped in elevators for hours. The Governor of New York declared a state of emergency. For a while it was unclear whether the accident had been caused by an attack or a failure of long-distance lines that had escalated into a disaster. News of this was brought by messengers across the narrow strip of turf between the orchestra and the first row of seats to the assistant sitting on the President's right, then by mouth to the latter's ear.

Only a few moments later, before the singers had launched into what was meant to be a humorous potpourri, the President's security advisor entered the scene with inappropriate haste, knelt down at Jimmy Carter's feet and conferred with him in this posture (Brzezinski is a tall man) about a dangerous state of affairs (the other guests only learned the reason for the conversation and its content later on): there had been an exchange of fire with a U.S. warship in the sea off North Korea; a Soviet ship had been involved. The question was whether this constituted a provocation that required a military response. In terms of possibly triggering a war, Zbigniew Brzezinski told the President, it was just as dangerous to react to fire from an insufficiently identified side as it was to show weakness and cause an escalation for that precise reason. So the result was almost the same whatever one decided, the President replied, as it was risky either way. Impossible, the Federal Chancellor rudely interjected after listening to them; one option was never as dangerous as the other, there was always a third way. A response was needed quickly, the security advisor exclaimed; every further word or argument was wasting time. Would it be better to make the wrong decision than to waste time? the President asked reluctantly.

The President, who was not interested in the music, still pretended in front of the guests that he was listening. In the present situation, he was unable to contribute anything in response to the urgent questions that were conveyed to him. The operetta by Sullivan from 1929, at any rate, did not contain any clues to solving political problems. For a moment, Carter weighed whether he should get up from his chair and summon his staff to the rooms of the White House. Interrupting the program would have been a dramatic step, itself a preliminary decision that a decision by the U.S. President was imminent. Now three military men also brought the news that U.S. citizens in Iran had been taken into custody in addition to the embassy staff who were under siege by the country's authorities. At that moment, there was daylight on the other side of the planet. Events were rushing along while America lay down to sleep.

Is there anything bothering you, Mister President? Federal Chancellor Schmidt politely asked. Nothing worth mentioning, the President replied. But the troublemaker Brzezinski, completely in his conspiratorial element, was still hovering close to the President's ear and speaking insistently to him. For the guests, the situation was unclear. Sullivan's operetta dealt with a billionaire's daughter who could not bring herself to divorce a boy in Brooklyn whom a schemer had accused of being UNFAITHFUL to her. It was unclear, as the singer explained, whether he loved another or only her—having repeatedly promised her the latter. This remained the problem until the end of the performance.

Lament of the Goods Left on the Shelf

A purchase transaction lasts 30 seconds. On average, the consumer makes a decision within seven seconds. Two-thirds of decisions are made in the supermarket itself. These are facts from market research.

Hunter societies developed their intelligence on game trails. In the marketing mix, packaging is the last bridge to the customer. Within the final seven seconds—which decide the fate of the item—the packaging must take its effect, without upsetting the consumer's preparatory measures of the previous 30 seconds and the approximately ten minutes comprising arrival and hesitating movements through the store. An acutely active spearhead must be linked with a plump softness or bluntness. The desire for the single commodity must not destroy the mood and suggestiveness of all of the commodities.

0.0005% of poets and thinkers on the globe are informal collaborators who work on the marketing mix. The distribution of maximized imaginative power on the planet is a matter of the organizational ability of 0.01% of organizers. These findings were made by Martians.

In the supermarket itself, expired products are nudged to the front, fresh products to the back. Each item must have its chance—even if, thanks to its expiration date, it is mortal.

This battle for the customer's seven seconds of attention is just as wide as it is deep. It occurs on a daily basis.

Ennio Morricone composed a requiem for failed commodities. Impulse buys require an agitator. The power of the brand name mustn't be upstaged by the special signaling of the packaging.

How forlorn is the packaged good that must be sent back, that must be destroyed. What is a population of cattle harboring one with mad cow's disease compared to a market that must be cleared on Saturday at 4 p.m. Nothing on the shelves can hope to be sold on Monday morning.

This thought moved Wolfgang Rihm as he spooned up noodles in the Restaurant Borchert in Berlin—that is to say, as he soothed the cells of his frustrated stomach walls after a rehearsal at the opera on Unter den Linden. These wolfish cells advised him to compose a lament for department store wares that have been declared unfit for consumption. He thought of the cook's scene in Monteverdi's *Il ritorno d'Ulisse in patria*. He'd memorized the exquisite melody, as was his wont. It created variations in his head all on its own. Every evening, this cook had exquisitely fed the suitors who were squandering Odysseus's fortune and beleaguering Penelope. To repeat: on someone else's dime. Now, after the murder of the suitors, after Ulysses—following an absence of 20 years—had once again claimed his Ithaca, he was being taken out of circulation—a discarded item, a cook who has taken leave of his things. He did not want to go on living like that. "The cook of the great Pompey looked like the great Pompey himself." Pompey died by his own hand, the cook by his own decision. Monteverdi never wrote a graver lament based on a side plot than he did about the cook who wished to die. Never did Wolfgang Rihm compose subtler funeral music than that which he wrote for *his* side interest—a bottle labeled "Dyspio" (whatever it might contain) that he passed by without buying. As he strolled past in the Galeries Lafayette, it had sent out its signal. He hadn't reacted fast enough. Maybe it was a perfume, maybe a beverage. In any event, a commodity. Now the informative lightning bolt—which never intended to end up in the head of a composer—lodged in Rihm's brain and from there brought about a lament that reached top spot in the magazine *Theater Today*—directly across from the Stuttgart opera house's top spot as the best opera house for three years running.

Alcina's Implacable Sadness

Nature as such, uninhabited and devoid of human guests, is bleak. So, too, the island on which the sorceress Alcina lives— originally an inhospitable rocky isle, an "old, terrible sight," as ugly as the rock to which the Valkyrie was banished.

Yet Alcina, granddaughter of Circe, inventive sorceress, is able to transform human souls into animals, brooks, green meadows, and lovely fields. And so, the island appears "inhabited." In her "underground sorcery chamber with various magical instruments and objects" she directs "pale shadows." But what sorcery! The psychic forces killed in Affect Theater are the fuel of a fairy-tale illusion. People do not seek the truth, said Petrarch, they fabricate illusions. They live blissfully in cocoons and do not catch cold from circumstances that bode ill for them.

The gods disappeared. The theater machines gathered dust. They could not hold out against sentiment. But now even sentiment is stripped out. The magical construction collapses, and the old witch Nature shows her rocky face once more, the power of water that washes everything away, the mad beauty of swamps and deserts.

Ruggiero, a soldier. As soon as he emerges from the cocoon of his capacity to love, he will die; he bids farewell to the green meadows of illusion: "Verdi prati." War is the agent that breaks the sorceress into pieces. She did not bewitch her lover, and when she loses him, it rips her apart. She sends beasts of prey after the unfaithful lover to tear him to shreds, but the beasts tear her to shreds, instead—as a sorceress, however, she won't die from it. "You pale shadows, you have revealed yourselves to be deaf." She throws away her magic wand.

Ruggiero, hitherto a deserter, returns to his regiment. Confronted with such self-sacrifice, the military justice system can't think of anything better to do than convict him of desertion and execute him.

Recently, not far from the Brandenburg Gate, in a garden that once belonged to the Liebermann Palace, a MEMORIAL TO THE UNKNOWN DESERTER was erected. At the opening ceremony, "Ah, mio dolor" (from Act 2, scene 8 of Handel's sorcery-opera *Alcina*) was played in its orchestral arrangement. The voice of Alcina was denoted by twelve first violins amplified with microphones. The memorial arrived more than a hundred years too late. In future wars, people won't be able to even flee. "Conquered, disenchanted Alcina!"

> *Del pallido Acheronte*
> *spirite abitatori*
> *e della notte ministri di vendetta*
> *cieche figlie crudeli,*
> *a me venite!*
> *(Act 2, scene 7)*

Lament for the Death of the Improbable

The singer of the VALKYRIE from six weeks ago girds herself in a breastplate for the overture of *Fidelio*. A soul like a fist. Defying the myrmidons, she will rescue her companion, now placed in her care.

In fact, her actions are naïve: she dresses up like a man but otherwise has no clear plan; she's just looking for a chance to get in on the action. She is seeking a *field of employment* for the task of liberation. She deceives people who trust her, instrumentalizes the androgynous powers of attraction she now possesses through her clothing. With a fair amount of luck, at the decisive moment, she becomes a participant in a murder scene and therein finds her battleground.

Her husband, Florestan, is being threatened by the unscrupulous prison warden, who's holding a pistol to his temple; Leonore threatens the warden with her own weapon. A deadlock ensues, the execution falters. The prison staff, momentarily confused, acts collectively as a referee.

Ah, if only such moments of equilibrium could last forever! But in the Stuttgart staging, the two fateful shots are fired at the same time.

So only the idea of the good survives, the fame of the help-meet who wanted to liberate her consort at any price—even at the price of her life and his. A lament for the POWER OF THE PROBABLE. Now the armored woman can only weep over her companion, set up the funeral pyre.

Are we none the wiser? The music and the stage directions for the mourning of Florestan, and for such an ending—the key to any new beginning—are actually to be found in the finale of the fourteen-hour opera, Wagner's *Der Ring des Nibelungen*, that played six weeks earlier. But that grandiose ending was sung by another singer of the Brünnhilde, alone on stage, without any décor or people around her. In this sense, we could say that in each case the torch of freedom is passed on and tossed forward in a kind of relay. What luck if, against all probability, the funeral pyre doesn't catch fire and we manage to avoid a global confla-gration—even if we didn't manage to protect our best friend!

The Resurrection of Musical Theater Out of the Spirit of the Sciences

At the opening of the Duke of Ferrara's collections, THEATRUM NATURAE ET ARTIS, an orchestra played. The plebeians gladly performed this service for the aristocrat in exchange for money, writes the critical spirit Dr. Schmiedhelm Weber, born in 1942, now in a holding pattern. The same singers sang who would, the following evening, be rehearsing their IL RITORNO D'ULISSE IN PATRIA. In the ensuing weeks and years, they could have continued to play in the duke's collections, which displayed monsters, skeletons, wax reliefs of human innards, and painted anatomies, but they did not, and so science was uncoupled from music, technical wonders from musical accompaniment, music from living practice. We observe here, along with Marx, noted Dr. S. Weber, a wrong decision. But nothing in the world is preventing us from going back the same way and repeating this stage, minus the mistake!* As such, history (as a cycle) is never completed. I received no applause, Weber writes, when I came to this conclusion in my lecture. I receive as little applause for my insights in my own former East Germany as I do in the former West Germany; not even in the adult education center of Tübingen did I get any response to my theses. My remarks, said an audience member, were as unscientific as they were unartistic. At the same time I know that history, and especially the history of music, is a system of tubes and caves in which one can move both forward and backward, an unfinished system of catacombs, like the burrows of beavers or marmots.

> *Once, as I danced,*
> *I came to Jerusalem—*

In private, by the light of a meager candle, with curtained windows, the doctors open up the dead, penetrate with their scalpels into the INNERMOST MYSTERIES. These studies lack both a public and a song.†

A group of astronomers, freezing in the clear winter night on their seats in a lonely tower. Galileo telescopes the miraculous timepiece that we planet-dwellers possess: the movements of the four large moons of Jupiter. But where are the choirs, the four orchestral voices for these moments of discovery? Meanwhile,

---

* Karl Marx, *Early Writings*: "The way out of alienation is always the way into alienation."

† The high ratings of the anatomy and death-cult shows recently added to the reality TV offerings by the station RTL 2, as verified by my colleague Dr. Ulrike Sprenger, reflect the greedy interest that audiences have contained within themselves for 400 years: without music, this interest remains coarse.

in every planetarium (from 6 in the morning till 3 at night) we repeat, music-less, Galileo's cold joy.

Or the ravishing DUTCH OPTICS: "OPTICKS," Newton's publication is entitled. What does the draftsman see through the ground glass? Samples of his saliva, music-less, and within them tiny animals—monsters. He knows that such creatures destroy his teeth, daily he cleans his biting-tools with a cloth, makes an effort to keep them in good shape. Radical discoveries long for a collective will engendered by music.

The human being befriending itself. Philanthropy, allocated to the products of science, befriending nature: how is that supposed to work (volumes 4, 5, and 6 of my commentaries discuss this, writes S. Weber, but the publisher Suhrkamp rejected them) without the participation of both hemispheres of the brain—one of which is inaccessible without the means of music? With this perspective (workforce and song arts of 350 years), it would not have been necessary to obliterate the German Democratic Republic through annexation. Indeed, the GDR wouldn't even have come into being as an actually existing thing in the first place. Despite Hanns Eisler, from the very beginning it lacked one thing: music.

I cannot understand how humanity can allow its most powerful force, that of the singing voice—which we call music—to be wasted on mediocre theater plays or religious prejudices (called "operas" or "oratorios"). Imagine if music had accompanied progress! Music and emancipation! Music and knowledge! Fascinated, "indeed, as if obsessed, the enemy soldiers crouched down and listened to the music broadcast by the loudspeakers. Not for that moment only did they forget the battle." This occurred in the confusion of the combat around Sedan in 1940.

Three years of waiting, then dropped. Landed in a dacha in Mecklenburg-Western Pomerania. My library, still unpacked, is sitting in a nearby barn. In Russia, my name would be known. In the world-republic, no one knows who I am.

At least the books, unread by me, are protected from rain, snow, and theft. I worry that predatory thieves who have no use for the books and who are unaware of their worth will destroy them in a rage over the uselessness of their booty. I've affixed three padlocks to the barn.

From my meager pay, which has already been cut many times, I save what I can for travel expenses. I attend international congresses. In my only decent suit. I deliver my lectures. Whatever my point of origin, it takes me twelve hours (with my bicycle and on foot) to get from Berlin's main station back to my hideout.

My research area: I am writing the 18-volume commentary to the preface to the *Grundrisse: Foundations of the Critique of Political Economy* (rough draft). This preface comprises seven printed pages. But what I'm after is what's in the gaps. What differentiates Hercules from a *joint stock company*? This is still a crucial question. As long as Hercules puts his powers to the test, he incorporates globalization.

Doesn't your exhaustiveness go a bit too far, esteemed comrade Schmiedhelm, people ask me?

It doesn't go nearly far enough! I would like to explain this using a simple example: in 1632, things came within a hair's breadth of turning out very differently. To repeat: the same orchestra played, and the same singers sang, for the opening of the collection of the ducal THEATRUM NATURAE ET ARTIS, who had earlier rehearsed an iteration of the myth of the return of Odysseus (with music). No one knows whether the myth is reporting something that really occurred. THEATRUM NATURAE ET ARTIS, however, exhibited *actual* unusual births (bona fide monsters), real inventions, and machines. At night, spectators paid an entry fee to watch corpses torn up, sewn back together, carried away: autopsies seeking the secrets of the body. Here, I would have suggested that they bring in soothsayers from antiquity, who would have handled the innards with more care, and more cheerfulness about the future. There were still some in Ferrara, 54th-generation soothsayers. And musical accompaniment would have set the human senses of both spectators and anatomists in motion.*

> *The goal is to make the petrified objects dance*
> *to their own melody—*

The natural sciences as a consequence of social ferment, social ferment as a consequence of the art of song, the indomitable longing people feel to make their surroundings flow, only by means of music, but not by music alone, also with sentiment as it expresses itself in action, but the latter as scientific action—this *is* (and not only "would be") the way of opera.

And be it not yet embarked upon, it is still my purpose, at pathologists', physicists', and astronomers' congresses, but also in talks before the directors' conference of the German Theater and Orchestra Association, to urge that this project—begun one day in the year 1632—finally be completed. The history of humanity is not such that we can say: because something was so, so must it remain.

---

* Karl Marx: "In practice, human senses behave like theoreticians." As, first, the labyrinthine ear.

"Dass ich das Liebste,
das ich habe,
töten muß .."

"That I must murder that
which I hold most dear..."

V "When We Were Still Reptiles, We Did Not Have Feelings"

Small-Statured Woman in High-Heeled Shoes

The opera singer rushes by. Tonight she will sing the role of To-sca. Because she is small and heavyset, she is wearing high-heeled shoes.

Internally, unnoticed, she is wearing an even smaller feeling: YOU'RE JUST ABOUT TO FALL OVER.

This feeling lies hidden beneath the passionate abandon, the murderous intent in the moment of hopelessness proper to the role of Tosca; and it is concealed by the feelings of Aida, which she sang last season. Still, the feeling possesses power, force, and ancestry.

When we were still reptiles, we did not have feelings, we understood only action. Resting—waiting—attack or flight.

Then came the Ice Ages. As it grew very cold on the blue planet, we often thought longingly of the primordial oceans, 98.6 degrees. We learned to have feelings, namely, to say: too hot, too cold.

To distinguish between the two, and to long: those are the two things feelings can do. Everything else is a combination.

My grandparents were simple farmers. Up to the birth of Christ, 64 billion ancestors. Each of these ancestors is related to a tree-climber to which all forebears can be traced back, and whose every feeling—falling asleep, tastes good, biting, oh dear, etc.—derives its FAMILY TREE from a single feeling-pair: hot/cold.

As it grew colder, Adam's rib was simply outsize longing.

Ninety-eight-point-six degrees in the warm waters of the primordial seas. We couldn't forget it, we remembered it in the cold,
we kindled this little fire in our interiors. The fire's antecedents
are the oscillations in the colors of atoms. In this sense, music is
older than feeling.*

Is Revolution Founded on Work or Ideas?
The Ghostliness of Revolutionary Processes

A colleague from the multifarious consulting firms of Roland
Berger, currently busy auditing the insolvent companies of a large
media empire, occupies himself in his free time (which is scant)
with topics that had been important to his life plans thirty years
earlier. Politically speaking, he emerged from a group that called
itself REVOLUTIONARY STRUGGLE, based in north Frankfurt.
Edwin Fuhrmann's nature, however, is so tenacious that in 2003
he was still keeping track of issues raised by REVOLUTIONARY
STRUGGLE's competing organizations; he was convinced of the
collective responsibility (similar to the contingent liabilities of a
general partnership according to §§128, 130 of the German Commercial Code) of all revolutionaries, regardless of which group
they belong to, for the duration. One cannot, he felt, agitate for
an idea and then let the inner passion to actually carry it out
simply fade away.

---

* In the nucleus of an atom dwell three colors, unremarkable so long as
they are together. Indifferent, uneventful. But if one of these colors were
pulled just a few millimeters away from the others, LONGING would
pull them all toward each other with energies sufficient to illuminate
the planets for about three weeks; and this is just one of the numerous
subatomic particle types that make up the elements.

Fuhrmann's question was as follows: was Mao Tse-tung really the monomaniacal tyrant he was portrayed to be in the memoirs of the victims of the *Cultural Revolution*? Was the *Cultural Revolution*—a failure by general consensus—an arbitrary campaign of violence? Will it recur? Can we learn anything from it? Fuhrmann found out that in the archives of the People's Republic of China, all documents pertaining to the *Cultural Revolution* are kept classified.

Now, the analytical methods used in company audits, as Fuhrmann knows them, have improved since 1989. Even vast processes like the Chinese *Cultural Revolution* can be described using auditing categories.

In an interview with the *Financial Times*, Fuhrmann made the following remarks:

FINANCIAL TIMES: Did the Cultural Revolution come from the periphery, from the center of China, or from below?

FUHRMANN: It was the result of highly explosive "good will."

FINANCIAL TIMES: Occasioned by what?

FUHRMANN: By the reform of Chinese opera and operetta (into the "political musical"). These cultural products built up a stronghold of idealism, which stirred up emotions.

FINANCIAL TIMES: And what came from the periphery?

FUHRMANN: A flow of raw materials, because young people (born after 1949) insisted on being involved. They had participated neither in the war nor in the beginnings of the revolution.

FINANCIAL TIMES: And what was added from the center?

FUHRMANN: The ideas of Mao Tse-tung.

FINANCIAL TIMES: So, twice we have ideas. From the opera and operettas, and from Mao Tse-tung?

FUHRMANN: Right. In China the question was, how could they avoid the alienation via technocratic processes that we know from the Soviet Union?

FINANCIAL TIMES: Earlier you asked: how can one keep a revolution that has eliminated substantial social ills (for example, forty million opium addicts were forcibly weaned from the drug) in revolutionary motion?

FUHRMANN: Trotsky called this the problem of PERMANENT REVOLUTION. To begin with, how can we retain the technical intelligence—on which every revolution, every advance depends—in the revolutionary process?

FINANCIAL TIMES: Has it been solved?

FUHRMANN: Not in the least. By the end, all political structures were destroyed. What remained was the dictatorship of the tripartite committees.*

FINANCIAL TIMES: Whose fault was it?

FUHRMANN: There are no judges in revolutions.

FINANCIAL TIMES: Can revolutions be repeated?

FUHRMANN: Definitely.

FINANCIAL TIMES: Was it the ideas that were wrong, or their execution?

FUHRMANN: An excess of ideas vis-à-vis reality is certainly wrong.

FINANCIAL TIMES: Could it have been avoided?

FUHRMANN: You mean, should one have had no ideas?

FINANCIAL TIMES: No—should one have taken a wait-and-see approach? If we are surprised by the result, does that mean we now understand better the ideas we had then?

FUHRMANN: That's more like it.

---

* In light of the upheavals at the end of the *Cultural Revolution*, tripartite committees were formed, uniting one representative each from the REVOLUTIONARY GUARDS, the PARTY, and the PEOPLE'S ARMY into a dictatorial governing body.

Christoph Schlingensief

The Complete Version of a Baroque Idea from Christoph Schlingensief

Jewish graves from the twelfth century bear the emblem of a hare. Oberrottenführer Hartmut Mielke noticed the symbol on the stones when his column leveled Jewish cemeteries in Central Germany in 1943 so that water tanks for fire engines could be set up there. The motif is repeated on seventeenth-century gravestones: prone, "sleeping" or "slain" hares.

This, as the Oberrottenführer knew—he was a local historian in peacetime—contrasted with the heathen portrayal of hares in the Celtic area south of the Rhön. There, hares are documented on sacrificial stones, not on graves.

The cousin of Friedrich Ludwig "Turnvater" Jahn, Alfred-Erwin Jahn, described in the *Zeitschrift für deutsche Vorzeitforschung,* volume 14, pp. 143 ff. (1809), the collision of the hare as a fertility symbol (as the spring myth of the goddess Ostara) with the "theatricalism of Golgatha": "the sorrowful farewell of the Son of God for a long time."

This passage inspired Richard Wagner's "Good Friday Spell," which he inserted into Act 3 of *Parsifal*. The pain of the cross and the cheerfulness of "vernally laughing nature" struck him as suitable contrasts to express the "straining of compassion."

The scenery conceived by Wagner from this perspective was now taken up by Christoph Schlingensief in his Bayreuth production of *Parsifal*. He had spent a long time searching in the score and texts of the piece for something that truly touched him.

In a basement of Humboldt University in Berlin, a dead hare, acquired in a specialty shop for game meat, was given over to the process of decay for several weeks. Walter Lenertz set up a 35mm Arriflex camera with a time-lapse apparatus. The light was adjusted. It was ensured that there were flies in the small chamber. The camera filmed the decomposition with time leaps over a space of several weeks.

An insight from Walter Benjamin's study *The Origin of German Tragic Drama* was confirmed. There Benjamin discusses a metaphor that is rather unpalatable in daily life: the hairy animal body being broken open by living, liquefied forces operating inside, so-called worms. The skeleton emerges. It was this kind of "dying nature," which already had "new life forming hastily" within it, that the time-lapse camera presented. It transpired that Benjamin was right when he called the "forward-thrusting intensity of maggots of different sizes in the ruined landscape of the expired hare" distressing.

The sight of the decomposing hare in a large-scale projection during the 'Good Friday Spell' caused the festival audience in Bayreuth some difficulty. They were not, after all, watching the "resurrection" of a hare, but rather the "continuation of life in the forms of decay": others living off what has died. By the end the hare had dissolved and worms were writhing, likewise "moribund," because the basement held no further food for them after consumption of the hare. That was DIFFICULT TO BEAR AS A MEANS OF ENTERTAINMENT FOR AN EVENING, but apt as a contribution to finding the truth.

At the international press conference after the dress rehearsal, Schlingensief defended himself against the accusation that his concept was "pessimistic." He could not see anything pessimistic or optimistic about the maggots' greed for life shown by the camera. Rather, it was a *positive* thing that the camera was capable of recording such a thing, enabling the events to be repeated time and again in the minds of future observers. What was "rebirth" if not something like that! "Overcoming of the overcomer." The seriousness of the music proved that; something of that kind could not be presented without shocks. Wagner's notes, tamed by Pierre Boulez, could not alleviate the shock.

A Second Titanic

As fires laid waste to the city, the opera in Smyrna continued to play its repertoire. The impresario Colonel Shubalov (head of the St. Petersburg Ballet, escaped Russia post–1917, later director of the Smyrna opera) could think of no better way to protect the valuable ensemble than to play an opera or operetta from start to finish each evening. If only not to appear to be "desperate prey." In the boxes and the orchestra sat Turkish cavalry officers. What better protection for the opera house?

As long as the performances took place in French, the Turks—who belonged to the upper classes—could follow the plot. They regarded it as an honor to be invited to such a cosmopolitan entertainment. During the day, the master carpenter and stagehands worked tirelessly to put together the sets so that they would in no way provoke the occupying powers (for example, in Mozart's *The*

Abduction from the Seraglio). The ballet corps and the sopranos had come from St. Petersburg as part of the wave of immigration resulting from the October Revolution. The wooden lining of the auditorium imitated that of the State Opera House in Budapest. Enchanting acoustics, if only because the temple of art had been wrought from wood—though it was also a fire hazard.

Those in Smyrna who wished to keep themselves and their loved ones safe showed up for these performances. Only in such surroundings—from orchestra seat to orchestra seat, from box to box—were the Turkish commanders approachable. They generously promised writs of protection.

It was an attempt, in extreme circumstances, to form a kind of SOCIETY. Until then, among tradesmen, this had not been necessary. One had gone to the opera or operetta merely to amuse oneself. Now, under the murderous regime of the Turkish military divisions, the convention of listening to musical dramas or following cheerful musical nonsense in ceremonial uniform represented a LAST REFUGE. It was clumsy workers, not the Turkish occupying force, who caused this "steamship of civilization" to burn. The Smyrna opera house became an expanse of rubble for other reasons than did the rest of the city. The Turks were not punishing the opera; they were punishing the pride of the Greeks.

–Count Shubalov, why didn't you manage to save this admirable temple of art, though you came close?

—The Smyrna opera is neither smaller nor less beautiful than the opera in Paris.

—Yes, but it still burned down.

—For no compelling reason.

—That's what's so tragic about it.

—It destroyed my self-confidence. I believed that I could save the steamship.

—Did you see the danger coming?

—Of course. And I went out to meet it. To establish a relationship of mutual trust with the supreme command of the Turkish cavalry division . . . that's not easy for a Russian. But for an aristocrat who has been expelled by the Soviet revolutionary government, the commander of a ballet corps, it's not impossible. Nothing so beguiles the Turkish cavalry officers as a confirmation that they belong to European civilization. They believe themselves to be Europeans.

—Which the Greeks dispute.

—For the Turks it's the other way around—it is the Greeks who are the barbarians. Ship-sinkers.

—And themselves?

—Children of a future Europe.

—Domiciled in Byzantium?

—Domiciled in the opera house of Smyrna. This was their encounter with a "European salon." They were delighted.

—They had the power, too. And so why were you not able to protect this valuable building?

—The wood that imitated the Budapest opera house burned like tinder. What we doused were stones. The stones are still standing.

—And a reconstruction?

—At the moment, the foreign currency for that is lacking.

Cavalleria Rusticana, an Opera about Strangers' Lives

A slight Sicilian is set to marry, per his mother's wishes, a young woman named Santuzza. However, he is not cut out for romantic relationships, and is more likely to be found seeking salvation with his pals in taverns than conjugally coddling a woman. Nevertheless, when the honor of his betrothed is besmirched by the all-powerful carter Alfio's inflammatory words, he must defend her. Yes—as a sign of bold defiance he must bite the ear of the physically superior carter. Then, in the duel, he will let himself be killed.

For Santuzza, this solves nothing.

In none of its particulars did this plot pertain to the doctor (an autodidact) who accompanied the soprano on his violin. The singer, accompanying herself on the piano, sang Santuzza's scene. Afterward, both played the intermezzo. He, the doctor, would never have bitten a stronger man in the ear. He would have found avenues of escape. He was a city person.

VI *Blast Furnaces of the Soul*

One Morning, Seven Days after my Fifth Birthday

My fifth birthday, 1937. My mother is very pregnant, in her eighth month. A week later, news reaches her of her father's death. She sits at the secretary in the study, cries, writes letters, "works off her grief"—but the tears still flow, unconsoled. When she has recounted the details often enough, written down the particulars in enough letters, the incomprehensible fact that she is now fatherless will be integrated into her new life.

She's not completely alone. I'm loitering around the gas fireplace. Over it is a bookshelf on which sits a red morocco-bound set of Shakespeare's *Collected Works*. Five years old, I can't read the books. I can write my first name in capital letters. The volumes, part of my mother's dowry, were imported from Berlin to Halberstadt. She has never read the books, either. One can take the books down from the shelf, finger them. The paper is tissue-thin. Turning over the pages, one senses: a valuable possession, not to be compared with the rough paper of the illustrated magazines or the daily newspaper. Next to the multi-volume luxury edition sits a guide to opera.

In my concrete memory (that is, when I concentrate on my impressions and leave out what I only "know"), I cannot tell the two books apart. Even though the paper is different, the books sit beside each other over the warming fire. So that the PROMISE of the "guide to opera" (considering the reverence with which my father takes it from the shelf) and the respectful FINGERING of the Shakespeare *Collected Works* (when the books are dusted, it is done with conspicuous care), blur together. Near me sits a usually cheerful, now disconsolate mother, and thus, for me, more open and tolerant (I'm careful not to whine, try to escape notice entirely, so she won't send me away; it is a long, happy morning). And so my devotion to opera, the *gesamtkunstwerk* of plot and music, came about before I could read or knew much about operas. First comes the ranking of things whose worth is measured by parents, then come the things themselves.

Following the Voice Where It Wishes to Go

This singer possesses a voice that can express every emotional nuance between a whisper and a scream. But "possesses" is the wrong word, since this voice is such a subtle instrument that no one, not even she whose voice it is, can really master it. The singing *occurs*, it rushes up, surprising even her, and her voice is not an instrument, but a blessing. In conversation, this singer has a good sense of humor. While working, she is intently focused and appears to be "not of this world."

Not long ago, she played SENTA WITH THE POWDER KEG in a staging by Peter Konwitschny. Breathless in another way than after singing a long cantilena to the end, she dragged a keg to the middle of the stage. The Dutchman and his crew returned to their ship. The inhabitants of the Norwegian port city were in a tizzy. The keg had a fuse. Senta lit it. With the explosion, Wagner's melodrama fizzled out.

On another day, the singer must get her bearings as Kundry, in *Parsifal*. How can a fool, the pupil of an overwhelmed mother, be made "world-clairvoyant," as the composer would have it? A practical approach is more appropriate than, as the libretto stipulates, mysterious knowledge of the past. The young hero has an unpleasant character. He lacks empathy, is ruthless to animals and plagued by phobias. He is supposed to join the brotherhood of believers. Seducing him won't work. The singer thinks: it is not my republic being founded here.

She would rather sing the role of Parsifal. Since Syberberg's film, we know that in the second act, when Kundry kisses the chaste man, he transforms into a girl, switching "soul groups." If she could take over his person, she could set the hero straight. Best would be if she were to sing both parts and thus make a *single* character out of Kundry and Parsifal. But then the character would no longer be a character, but a living person.

The putting back together of separated components could turn the opera into a PROMISING COMPILATION; it could bring a "spark of hope" into the music house. If the singer had her way, no swans need die. The magician Klingsor would not have to die just because he, the outcast, is attracted by the brotherhood. Along with the elaborate sin, chastity would be annulled, two of humanity's blind alleys would fall away, and, from a bifurcation approximately 100,000 years ago, a lovely sequence of tendernesses and kindnesses would branch off. One should, said the singer in conversation with me, place the overture from *Rheingold* at the end of *Parsifal*, and finish with the first human voice, the call of the Rhinemaiden, greeting the glittering rays of the sun on the cool expanse of water.

The singer has always wanted to sing this keen sound from the primeval world. But she is so famous, and so in demand at all the great opera houses, that she is never offered such a minor part. She is too good for a Rhinemaiden, and even if she did get the role, she would never be able to focus on just this one sound— and she doesn't want to sing the entire role, she just wants to articulate this *one* cry. The only remaining option is to convince the musical director to add this inspired sliver of music from the *Rheingold* to the lugubriously male and somewhat miserable finale of *Parsifal*, although it would require the entire overture to be effective. She wouldn't expect applause—she'd expect delight. In her life as a singer, this woman will have about 7,600 evenings' worth of singing. For a few of the most beautiful minor matters in the body of opera literature, it is not enough.

"It was one romantic relationship, no superfluous words"

They couldn't exchange any words, since they did not understand each other's language. In the darkness of the stables where they were touching one another, it would have been foolish to hold forth. Far away, outside, the noise of the hunting party. They drank from small silver cups, unpacked their provisions from parchment paper. Thanks to a stable door padlocked from the inside, the two were cut off from the outside world. Though from different stations, they immediately felt close.

They were also concentrating far too much to be able to talk. Perhaps they could have made use of their words as they were using their hands, to touch each other with vocal expression (without having to make sense). But they didn't do so, because the fervor of the touching made them take leave of their senses. Members of the hunting party could have shaken the stable door—they would not have let themselves be disturbed. He had clutched at her as he unsaddled her horse. She had clutched at him. They had known each other for perhaps thirty minutes. It was as if they had broken through a hole in the floor of the Earth. No longer of this world. And they gave no thought to how they would ever reemerge—disheveled and, more to the point, unable to be seen together—from their vault. What they were doing was punish-

---

"It was one romantic relationship ..." is taken from a poem by Friederike Mayröcker.

able by law. He was a forced laborer.* The thought ran through her mind: I must not put him in harm's way. She was not indiscreet. But nothing could hold them back. Mutely, they panted.

"Temples of Seriousness"

In the nineteenth century a capital city, whether of a province or an entire country, requires a palace of justice, a stock exchange and an OPERA HOUSE. Architecturally they tend to be rather similar. The entrances often "surrounded by columns." Karl Kraus and Th. W. Adorno cite the opera houses in Lemberg and Budapest (the latter clad within entirely in wood like a violin) as examples of such "temples of seriousness."

There is, after all, hardly anywhere in such cities where COMMUNAL AND PUBLIC MOURNING is possible. Adorno couldn't imagine a performance of an opera in the open air or in a public place where all kinds of other movements might take place. Something inside me, he said, needs the painted dome above the auditorium as a dividing wall to separate it from the sky and anything it might throw at us.

Santuzza and Turiddu

A Sicilian farming village, Easter 1880, before mass. A young woman, Santuzza, goes to see Lucia, the owner of a wine shop and mother of her lover, Turiddu, to ask if she knows where Turiddu is. Turiddu has left Santuzza because he is in love with

---

* After 1940, the Third Reich requisitioned forced laborers from the countries they were occupying. Such workers were strictly forbidden from intimacy with German women.

Lola, the carter Alfio's wife. At this very moment, Alfio is returning to the village after a long trip. He is proud of his profession,
and also prides himself on his wife's fidelity. The villagers head
to church. Santuzza is waiting anxiously in the wine shop when
Turiddu appears. Lola sashays by; Turiddu makes toward her.
Before his military service, he had courted Lola, but ultimately
lost her to the carter. Santuzza blocks his path, pleading with
him to come back to her. He pushes her away. Santuzza's soul
sharpens like a knife. As Alfio walks by, Santuzza reveals to him
that Lola is cheating on him with Turiddu. Horrified by what she
has done, Santuzza runs off. At this point, the legendary INTER-
MEZZO plays before an empty stage.

After mass, the churchgoers stop in at Turiddu's mother's wine
shop. Turiddu, protected by his powerful mother, plays the host.
As he holds out a glass of wine to the carter, the latter bats it out
of his hand. "I'll be waiting for you outside, behind the garden,"
Alfio says coldly. Turiddu, who now regrets his imprudence, asks
his mother to protect Santuzza. Then he draws his sword and
rushes out. Ominous silence. A sudden cry: "Turiddu hath been
slain. Turiddu is dead!"

The opera is called *Cavalleria Rusticana* (farmer's honor). For
a few weeks in 1943, my father suspended his morning consul-
tation hours. Irma Hofer, soprano at Halberstadt's municipal
theater, accompanied him on the piano. She sang the role of
Santuzza, while he played the basic melodies on his violin. In
the vestibule, I sat very still and listened. This vestibule served
as the passageway from the kitchen and was also the abode of
the box on the wall with attached receiver, which constituted the
telephone. This part of the house was a kind of junction. It was
infused with the aura of my mother, who was constantly on the
telephone, noting down what needed to be fetched from the city
on scraps of paper kept here. An organizational headquarters,
now flooded with music. My children still laugh when I call the

telephone, a device that enables one to listen and speak across distances, a "Fernsprecher,"* or when I speak of the "exchange," as if telephone calls were still facilitated through people. But I'm still thinking of the box with the removable receiver described here, and for me the word "Ferngespräch" (talk across distances) is tied to the sound of the *Cavalleria Rusticana* intermezzo that the two were performing in the study. In a movie I saw as a ten-year-old, a pair of lovers keeps in touch on the day war breaks out in 1914 through just such a box on the wall. They talk about how they are now citizens of enemy countries, and how they will probably never see each other again. In the alchemist's laboratory of my soul, it is impossible for me to distinguish the degrees of importance of these phone calls I witnessed as a child, scanned with a key scene from a film that dissected romantic drama for me, and with passion (cool piano, heated violin, vivid voices).

Nights in Empty Opera Houses

In her films, my daughter Sophie does everything differently than I do in my films. But in one respect we're alike—she refuses to employ any dramatic plot, although she knows perfectly well that it would help with pitching projects and, ultimately, with success. She has no interest in the escalation of conflict that induces so-called suspense. Instead, she holds conflict itself in suspense. She enjoys watching. People seek each other's proximity, but then they separate. Nothing happens, and we watch.

On the other hand, my daughter says, something *does* happen, something one wouldn't normally understand as a "plot." For her, this is the camera work. Avoiding the EMOTIONAL TANGLE is

---

* Translator's note: an old-fashioned word for telephone, roughly translated: "distant-speaker."

the reason why for 90-minute films I've always preferred the circus's principle of "numbers" over any drama tied to plot. But then why am I so magically attracted to the opera, which almost universally practices the crochet-principle of plot escalation? This type of dramaturgy annoys me. I believe this is why I intuitively dissect every opera I hear (or, better: that I film) into its component parts. Beneath the threshold of the actions on stage, the fragments do follow the principle of "numbers," however much Richard Wagner might have striven to overcome it. The elements operate among themselves, they respond to each other (under the skin of the events).

I believe that at night these particles haunt empty opera houses, fighting and being affectionate by turns. A Leonore (from *Fidelio*) with a knack for rescue wanders into Verdi's *A Masked Ball*, reveals her knowledge of the plot to the protagonists, and clears up the fatal misunderstandings—just as she once rescued her husband Florestan from the dungeon.

"Déjeuner sur l'herbe" in the nighttime backdrop for "The doomed who were rescued": Werner Schroeter (when he visits me during such nocturnal hours in the opera house) objects to my heartfelt belief that the moment of greatest passion (which accepts death as a possible consequence) is not to be idolized in favor of day-to-day life in a conventional marriage or profession. I respond to his objection: You're wrong. People cohabiting over a long period of time—their living bodies, their spending time with their children, their fantasies, their work, their "little successes"—do not have to be humdrum.

In Bremen, a shipyard closes. The qualified man to whom Gerda Behnke once, with calm resolve, committed herself (for life, that was the plan)—they have two children—is forced to look for a new position in Baden-Württemberg. Husband and wife see each other rarely. In a moment of rashness, Gerda decides to go visit her husband in his provisional digs down south. The day before, her husband had met an attractive office worker in a suburban café who'd dropped hints that she might be approachable; for his part, he is not incorruptible. But thanks to Gerda's happy fancy, this thread of fate is quickly severed. Not long afterward, Gerda discovers she is pregnant for the third time. Trube, work-time analyst, specializing in averages that nevertheless encompass extreme fluctuations from the norm, has calculated the potential for happiness in Gerda's life. When compared with the happiness quotient in opera dramas, Gerda's amount of happiness proves to be the greater. The precision of Trube's reckoning is challenged by his colleague Giglatz. Both are of the opinion that true poets should also be statisticians. And both are sorry that no opera score—at least, as far as their summary examination has been able to determine—accords with the POETIC PRINCIPLE as they understand it.

In one of the opera characters' nightly encounters, which are beyond the control of the artistic director, the passionate Amneris, a contralto rebuffed in love, sets off for the hinterlands to incite married couples in Middle Germany to conduct more daring love lives: the idea is to export operatic energies to private households. In Verdi's *Aida*, this Amneris loves the young officer commanding the Egyptian army on a campaign against the "Ethiopian barbarians." But he loves only Aida, slave and prisoner of war, hardly Amneris's equal in rank. Amneris cannot comprehend this affront to her legitimate feelings—that is, receiving the opposite of respect and reciprocated love. At the end of the opera she wonders why three people can't at least live together, thereby attaining a more judicious distribution of the fulfillment of longings. In the consulting practice she sets up nights in the opera house's spirit realm, she advises all life-practitioners in the city to make NOVEL CONSTELLATIONS IN THE SEARCH FOR

HAPPINESS. Amneris calls for a court that would decide on such emotional questions. Verdi gave Amneris the more subtle music, a vocal armament against which the tenor and the victorious soprano are defenseless. At least Verdi's music is just, even if the plot celebrates injustice.

Madame Butterfly's Happier Cousin

In her second semester at an art academy in southern Germany, the daughter of a brewery owner (with properties in Bavaria, but also in the Czech Republic) met and fell in love with a Japanese man. This man was part of the academy's technical crew and had immigrated to Germany as an electrician (he came from a poor, landless family near Osaka). After some time, the unequal pair is in possession of two hoped-for children, a boy and his younger sister. Today, they are all having breakfast in a café.

In sharp contrast to her blue skirt, the young blonde woman is wearing a blood-red scarf around her neck, wound about three hand-widths high, a lavish decoration. Somewhat stiffly, her man in corduroys presides over the table. The children are wild—outside, they've misappropriated the signs listing the restaurant's offerings and have built a hut out of them.

The man from Japan goes to the men's room for a time. When he returns, the family prepares to leave. The man's movements are "practical," somewhat inelegant, almost technical. As they leave the café, he first places his daughter on his shoulders with his strong hands and then bends her around his midriff. She moves her young body accordingly, as though it were a circus act. The four of them are not aristocrats, the parents are not citizens of the same country, their social backgrounds are different, they don't belong to any of the known target groups, they have varying ways of dressing and moving their bodies, different skin colors and different allergies. In the children, this all got mixed together. They appear to be conflict-free.

Recently, at the Easter Salzburg Festival, the four went to see MADAME BUTTERFLY in a conventional staging, sung in Italian. The U.S. naval officer who plays such a fateful role in the opera's storyline was sung by a Japanese tenor. The Japanese woman seduced and then left in the lurch by this officer—traditionally called "Butterfly"—was sung by a woman from Birmingham who looked like a nineteenth-century English heiress.

The happy day-trippers, who had good seats in the festival hall (the young woman's bank account was regularly replenished by her brewery-owning father)—the children already tired in the evening, but patient and well-behaved in their seats—made fun of what was performed for them. They had no feeling for tragedy.

Misunderstanding between Two Worlds

As an experienced tenor, I would like to take a stand against the usual vilification of Pinkerton in Puccini's *Madame Butterfly*, whom I portray. One can certainly claim that Puccini so arranged this part musically that at the end of the piece, the audience doesn't forgive Pinkerton for the soprano's death. But that is not the situation in the first act, upon which my role is primarily built, vocally speaking. One cannot deny my performance a certain warmth, especially during the love duet. At all events, I put warmth into my voice. To position Pinkerton as a caricature of a lecherous U.S. imperialist who exploits an Asian woman seems to me an oversimplification.

I see the U.S. naval officer that I sing as the commander of a battleship. He gets involved with a lady from a Japanese noble family that has come down in the world. She has been professionally procured, as it were, like a hetaera in the ancient Greek sense.

He spends a few weeks of vacation time with her. He understands the so-called marriage of convenience to be a local custom. He does not suffer from a guilty conscience when he returns to duty and to the United States.

He only learns between the second and third acts that he has impregnated the young Japanese woman. Meanwhile, in the U.S., he has married into a family that will aid his advancement. His wife Kate, a cool Protestant, remains childless. After Kate learns of the child, she conceives of the idea of adopting it—not least to secure *her* marriage of convenience—and to that end travels with her husband to Nagasaki. This, at least, can't be held against the tenor. Due to my emotional involvement with the part of Pinkerton (I have by now sung this role, note for note, 386 times), I am certain that the knot of fate—the tragic self-directed aggression of the Japanese woman—is based on a vast misunderstanding between two cultures, a CLASH. At no point has this woman accepted the status of commercial service provider to which she saw herself forced after the death of her father and attendant loss of fortune. She barely understands what has happened to her. She possesses no "capitalist soul." The tenor was raised very differently. I see him as a vivid, lively, mercurial primate, who believes himself to be a lucky prince, the exponent of a highly modern fleet. What drives him, and what flows melodiously through my throat, is the spirit of accepting an advantage, to which all my senses—as well as a sort of accounts register in my honor code—subordinate themselves ("You must not neglect your advancement, you must not take a back seat to any rival"). This kind of drive can distract you. I also want to note that the paper marriage in the first act and the promises he sings occur in a drunken state, intensified by the intoxication of the prospect of love. Here, two people have found each other—their minds misunderstand each other, but their senses have conjoined. Before any international court of arbitration, with Japanese and Americans equally represented, Pinkerton would be absolved of guilt. He is not disloyal, either—though he might seem to be careless in his manner—for he always remains true to himself.

> *To die with honor,*
> *when one can no longer live with honor.*

This note, which the young Japanese woman leaves behind as a message for Pinkerton, must appear strange to me, the tenor. At this point in the drama, I show this by hesitating. I consider it to be an atavistic law that stands in opposition to my sensuous vocal delight.

The Birth of Tragedy Out of the Spirit of Renunciation

In the fall of 1941, time grew tight for me. In sixth grade at the cathedral school where I had been a pupil since Easter, I was having a hard time keeping up. The tutoring my mother had initiated immediately after the catastrophes of my first few weeks would only show results in the long term. In the midst of this fast-paced life, an Italian film dubbed into German and entitled *The Dream of Butterfly* played for fourteen days in the Kino Capitol, and was responsible for one of my most powerful early impressions in cinema. Eight days in a row, I attended each two o'clock screening (in the side loge, practically unable to see the screen, and only with the permission of the cashier Miss Schrader—children under 14 years of age were not supposed to be allowed in). The film is set in the period just after the original premiere of Puccini's *Madame Butterfly*.

The plot: before the opera singer Rosi Belloni (Maria Cebotari) can tell her fiancé, the music student Harry Peters (Fosco Giachetti), that she is expecting his child, he tells *her* that he has been offered a job in America. Thinking of his future, which she believes in, Rosi advises him to accept the offer. Years go by, and Rosi hears nothing from Harry Peters. She raises her child and matures into a great artist. At her request, the premiere of Puccini's new opera *Madame Butterfly* is held at Milan's Scala. Among the guests: the conductor of the Metropolitan Opera. Rosi recognizes Harry Peters. She learns that he is married. In addition, she notices that his trip to Milan is about the opera, not about her. Only now does Rosi recognize the peculiar similarities of her private fate with the opera's plot. She pours a harrowing intensity into the performance [close-up of the lovers in the opera's first act]. No word of reproach crosses Rosi's lips. FROM NOW ON, SHE BELONGS SOLELY TO HER ART AND TO HER CHILD.

Why Cinema Was Unable, Due to its Conditions of Production, to Become the OPERA OF THE TWENTIETH CENTURY

Theodor W. Adorno once had occasion to call Fritz Lang—not without a certain affection in his tone—his "kitsch brother." The epithet was not meant disparagingly, Adorno responded when I asked him about it. Otherwise, he added, he wouldn't have used the word *brother*. With this remark, he was referring to a certain audacity, brutality, or insouciance with which Fritz Lang—it was simply part of the film business—pruned material and opera-ready plots for use by the public and his direction. Lang had been applying this methodology—especially to films, which he considered by-products—since his early period. It would be wrong to think that he started doing so during his time in Hollywood. Adorno's comment referred specifically to a silent film entitled *Harakiri* that Lang had directed in 1919 as the "second film of the Decla world class" in Berlin. The movie made use of material from Puccini's *Madame Butterfly*. Lang chose a version that ignored the sense of the opera.

The Japanese father of a young, exotic woman (called O-Take-San in the film), a merchant out of a Lessing play, returns from Europe and showers his beloved daughter with gifts, including costume jewelry and a teddy bear from London. The village priest, guardian of the Yoshiwara shrine in Nagasaki, views the foreign presents as a contamination of the village and a religious infraction. These accusations induce the father to commit hara-kiri. The daughter, however, is to serve the monk as "under-priestess." In "Buddha's Holy Garden" she meets a Dutch naval officer, and they enter into a "999-year pact." A kind of charade. But the Dutch man is only using O-Take-San. After he returns to Holland, he does not keep in touch. Many years later, the sailor comes back to Japan. Accompanied by a European wife. Thereupon the exotic beauty throws herself upon her father's sword.

The aim of the plot, as Adorno commented, was to avoid copyright infringement of Puccini's original material. This sacrificed much of the sense and many of the emotionally comprehensible situations. Lang focused on parallel montages—of the group of temple guards, and of the collective of seducers in the Dutch naval club. The interior of the temple in which the religious turnkeys live was tinted dark brown, the teahouse and officers' mess glaring yellow. (Fassbinder emulated this coloring method in his final films, even though the era of black-and-white films was past.) Adorno asked: could music have saved Fritz Lang's 1919 film?

An Archeologist of Opera

As a paleoanthropologist and archeologist and—my side job— an opera connoisseur, I have become something of an expert in train and plane schedules. *You* try to get from an archeological site in Syria (during periods in which I am not needed at the excavations) to orchestra dress rehearsal 2 in Oslo, and from there to a premiere in Naples. I cannot leave the excavation site unsupervised for long: I have to get back quickly. When one is absent from the site, one quickly loses control over it. Artifacts are swiftly purloined or traded, or they fall into the hands of the local despots. My assistants don't have my same authority.

So, first the leg to Aleppo, then a bus to the airfield in Jordan, change planes in Rome, and the rest of the way to Oslo in the blink of an eye. Because of the nighttime flight ban, I cannot make use of the nocturnal hours. This kind of travel demands my total concentration on the route, on being punctual, on making the connections. From Naples, another side trip: piano rehearsal of Jommelli's *Berenice, the Queen of Armenia* in Stuttgart. The newest production of my indefatigable excavation colleagues Jossi Wieler and Sergio Morabito.

Last week on our excavation site, we found ourselves briefly in the power of the CALIPHATE. Even before these militants realized what we were digging for, the ISLAMIC THEOCRACY (a somewhat less violent fraction of the Islamists) had freed us. Because even these warriors demanded a fee, we now pay protection money to a Druze organization, who in turn pay the militarily more powerful Islamists a lease for taking us on. An archeological site in Syria is as valuable as an oil well for the international weapons trade.

Whatever we excavate during the day, we bring to the coast the very same night, because the protection we are paying for is not reliable. But most of what we find we leave in the ground. The trade route proceeds through Cyprus, Russia, and Uzbekistan to Marseille and from there to Tokyo or the West Coast of the U.S., depending on where the end consumer is. I have sometimes lodged with armed colleagues in the port of Tartus. It is easier to intercept the good pieces there than to dig them out yourself and guard them on site.

My name is Dr. Sc. Fred Kaul. The name comes from Eisleben. My forefathers were geologists in Freiberg in Saxony. I took piano lessons for sixteen years. As a boy, I was thought to have talent. Now there is no proficiency left, just my love of my métier, my exploratory spirit. Although I am not yet old, my hands are gouty.

I'm often asked what I am seeking in opera houses, since I'm not very interested in the operas' plots or in the often unwieldy music. I tell the person asking that they ought to take a look at my notes. I judge the music based on its DEGREE OF SERIOUS-NESS, its "MELTING POINT." Nowhere, with the exception of a loved one's funeral, is mourning more impressive than in the orchestra pit of an opera house. As for what is happening on the stage, I am interested in the details. It is not the *plot* revealing the signs that refer to goings-on in the opera I would like to know about. The story is only the mask for it. The secret lies in the minor points of the action, in tiny fragments. When we excavate, we also rarely find the entire object from antiquity—just splinters and remnants that we fit together.

For example, in Verdi operas there are conflicts between men (tenors, baritones, bass). They fraternize with each other, they fall out, they exchange oaths, they take part in intrigues. They rarely kill each other in their fights; instead they kill a substitute (a woman, the soprano). I record all this in my notes, in addition to counting the shifts in the music, noting down how the music intensifies, the stresses on musical syllables. When after an oath of allegiance the fatally wounded tenor confesses his love for the soprano to his pursuer (the baritone), whom he considers his best friend, I must investigate what it really means. It's always something other than what is actually being shown. The key is in the focal calibration of the music.

As an archeologist, I am not surprised that what's really at is-sue are traces from remembered history that date back to the early period of humanity: let's say 60,000 to 9,000 years BC—the SCARS OF EMOTION FROM LONG AGO. Like magnets. They set the IMAGINATIONS OF COMPOSERS AND POETS IN A BRIGHT BLAZE.

As interest in opera waned throughout the twentieth century, the archaic attractors leaped over to reality, and the cities burned. My excavations are concerned with layers, and there are many more levels underneath the plot and the basic overall impression of the opera's music. I'll come back to this. Don't be fooled when a sleepwalker in Bellini's opera sings her often cheerful melodies while the grave (obvious to the audience) lies right in front of her. In all serious operas, the subtext is sacrifice, grief, bitter frag-ments of memory that are similar to the finds I bring up from the earth, and that speak more often of "history as slaughtering block" than of joyful celebrations.

—How is your method different from that of a lie detector?
—It isn't. Except there's no machine, just my ear as the measuring device.
—How do you propose to determine when music is lying?
—I'm an archeologist.
—Could the method you use for operas be applied to lighter entertainment—operettas?
—Operettas lie only a little. For my excavations I require con-centrated seriosity.

I "think" best, that is to say I concentrate best, when I'm travel-ing. As soon as I arrive at the excavation site, people start talking at me from all sides. There's no break. At night, when I stop di-recting the excavation, I am tired and crawl into my tent. But when after traveling I have reached my destination and have transported my ears to the opera house (I close my eyes), my attention is focused on something other than what I myself am thinking. While I am observing an opera, I must completely cut myself off from my own thoughts. Total listening is equivalent to the precision work of a geologist. I don't have to pay attention to the artistic labor on the stage or in the orchestra pit; I must simply let what is happening flow through me if I want to discover what it is that I as an excavator wish to secure.

"A Scarecrow of Religious Fury"

Heinrich Heine would happily have written the libretto for a dance-opera for Giacomo Meyerbeer. Instead, Eugene Scribe got the job. It was the Anabaptist opera *The Prophet*. Heine deemed Scribe's libretto "a crying shame."

The story takes place around 1536. The innkeeper Johann von Leyden must endure the fact that his bride Bertha (soprano) and his mother Fides (alto) have been imprisoned by the violent and lascivious Count Oberthal. It is unclear whether the count is abusing the women or wants to use them to blackmail the bishop of Münster. The innkeeper Johann, incited by three villainous Anabaptists (bass, baritone, tenor), lets himself be proclaimed a prophet. He storms Oberthal's fortress and conquers the city of Münster. He has himself crowned king in the cathedral ("Coronation March"). For the sake of his alleged divine provenance, he disowns his mother, Fides. His bride Bertha stabs herself.

In the end, Johann is betrayed by everyone. Put on trial, he has the courtroom blown up by his last two adherents. He dies, along with his friends, enemies, and mother.

Heine needed Meyerbeer's influence to write a letter arranging

for a close relative of Heine's in Hamburg—a banker—to transfer money to the poet. And so Heine was unable to publish the
hatchet job on the opera that he had already written.

From Heine's notes:

"The religious motive that Jean de Leyden dies for is replaced
by a garden-variety motive. Mother and wife, whom he does later
disown, are 'imprisoned.' He gets them back. There is no need
for him to accept dying like a martyr.

"By blowing himself up, Jean obliterates his sacrificial death.
What if Jesus, instead of dying on the cross, had vanished from
the world in a burst of theatrical thunder? Leaving behind a note
saying that he would be back soon? Would that have made him
the Savior?"

Can Hearts Set Buildings on Fire?

The notion that the fires of passion by which singers get carried away in the heat of an opera's climax—that is to say, fiery
souls—can actually set the building on fire is easily dismissed
as superstition (though it *would* explain the piling up of opera
house fires in the last decade of the nineteenth century, which
prompted Karl Kraus to call opera houses "our volcanoes in the
middle of the city"). This according to Witzlaff, investigator of
causes and catastrophes. He argues that if you look at the film
footage of the actions of the Cairo fire department during the
legendary conflagration at the Cairo Opera House (the building,
when new, was supposed to attract Verdi's *Aida* to the Egyptian
capital when the Suez Canal opened), you can see that it is the
incompetence of those extinguishing forces at fighting theater
fire that is responsible for the infernos, and not a "spark of song."
The Egyptian firefighters tried to tackle the fire with a single

hose after it had already taken hold of the foyer curtains and was leaping out of the high windows of the front building. The water in this sole firehose petered out. The firefighters then frittered away much time connecting a hose from the Old Town, where the opera house was located, to the Nile. When they returned to battle the fire with three hoses, the building had already burned to the ground. But the investigator's argument does not answer the questions prompted by Karl Kraus's remark.

The Fire at the Ringtheater

During one of his visits to Munich, Heiner Müller showed me a treasure he had found. He had brought it from Luigi Nono's Venice apartment, which he had rented for himself and his young bride on their honeymoon in that city. In a drawer, he said, he had discovered a fragment of written music. The notes, in Nono's handwriting (and with his characteristic arrows, insertions, and colors), concerned an opera project. The subject matter was the fire in Vienna's Ringtheater in the winter of 1887 (my maternal grandmother would have been fifteen years old at the time). The notes seemed sufficient for a performance of about twenty minutes. Müller was now planning a "drama with music" based on these fragments. The theme was short and compact.

During an evening performance of Offenbach's *Tales of Hoffmann*, before the barcarole, which always got the audience swaying to the music, a fire broke out and spread quickly throughout the labyrinthine building, whose emergency exits had been closed off by renovations so that it was essentially barricaded. The doors to the concert hall could only be opened from the outside, by the ushers—some of whom, however, were taking a break during the performance. The audience fought against these doors in the dark. On the terrified faces: a few glimmers of the amusement of the previous hour. 383 people burned to death.

Based on Nono's remarks and his own imagination, Müller had sketched out a series of seven scenes:

1. Scene: "The fire's source."
Orchestral interlude.
2. Scene: The doors' fastenings. Nono's precise information and dashed drawings, which show the locks' technical aspects. Ushers and experienced locksmiths explain their mechanism.
Orchestral interlude.
3. Scene: Excerpts from operas and operettas performed in the burned-down opera house. Time-lapse film with music.
Orchestral interlude.
4. Scene: Fugato on the text: "How could the performance have begun before a single prudent police officer had checked to make sure nothing could go wrong?"
Entracte buffone: Orchestra with narrator's voice.
5. Scene: "Hearts burn." For this image there were no further scenic indications, although Nono had set down a number of notes for singing voices in the draft score.
Orchestral interlude.
6. Scene: "No one wants to die in a pleasure palace."
7. Scene: "In the style of a *recitativo secco*: recital of the list of the dead at the Ringtheater fire. Narrator's voice."

Müller had written out the sequence of scenes on seven beer coasters. Obviously, he said, Nono's sketch was a fragment that required further elaboration. This was the work he hoped to devote himself to next. Like so many others, this project was interrupted by his illness.

When the Audience Heard the Familiar Melody, They Returned in an Orderly Fashion to Their Seats

One year after the end of the Franco-Prussian War, when gas candelabra lamps were still in use, during a performance of Halévy's opera *La Juive* a lagging feather on the hat of a girl in the chorus caught fire on a gas flame backstage. Other members of the chorus put out the fire at once, thoroughly stamping out the flames. Nevertheless, a trace of the smell produced by this incident penetrated the concert hall. A woman shrieked: *Fire!* The quick-thinking conductor had a fanfare played three times in a row. Shouts: *It's nothing! Quiet!* Just as the audience was finally settling back down, firefighters rushed into the hall. They wanted to help, but they only stoked the disturbance. At that moment, the conductor gave the cue for the interrupted piece to continue. When the audience heard the familiar melody, they returned in an orderly fashion to their seats.

Death of a Thousand Souls

Until his final days, Modest Mussorgsky managed to write music and to move his heavy hands over the piano keys. He was drunk at all times of the day. The confidants who looked after him lost all respect for the genius. It was in this state that the master composed the last act of his opera *Khovanshchina*. There were still gaping holes in the notations to the preceding acts: only the piano arrangement had been sketched out. Then Mussorgsky sank into death, drowned in ineffable despair.

The draft of the fifth act depicts the self-immolation of an old orthodox sect in Russia during the chaotic time of Peter the Great's accession to power. At stake for the religious group, who were considered fanatics, were rites that they on no account wished to see altered. A religious leader initiated the collective self-sacrifice. His medium was a trusted advisor who had the confidence of all, and who was in a position to call upon them to commit the act. She had once been a sorceress, and was also the discarded mistress of the leader of a troop of rebelling guardsmen ("Khovansky") whom she still loved, and to whom she had offered refuge in the sect's hideout in the woods. Trees were felled, logs stockpiled. You need lots of dry brushwood and other spontaneously flammable material for an auto-da-fé. A Russian forest with its fresh sap is not very well-suited to self-immolation.

The czar banned the Old Believers' rites. The sect remained obstinate. If Russia is ever to gain parity with the West, reasoned the czar and his advisors, an example must be set. Beliefs and rituals must be centrally unified and simplified for the comprehension of third parties. The idea of a UNIFIED TOP, which leads to progress, must be chiseled into the people's heart. This "heart" (made of many thousand souls and with no specific location in their bodies, and perhaps simply existing AMONG ALL PEOPLE) cannot, however, be hewn by force. The tool for it has not yet been invented (stone isn't suitable, nor are hammers, pestles, or smelteries).

The czar's troops surrounded the forest. Scouts for the besieged sect announced the approach of the czar's cavalry, at which moment the leader's confidante (the medium) gave the sign. Sticks covered in flammable material were pulled from the campfires and used to set the forest on fire. The Old Believers suffocated before they could succumb to the flames. When the czar's soldiers searched the forest, they were all already dead. The soldiers, trained only for parades and military drills, were baffled.

Stravinsky translated this part of the opera from Mussorgsky's piano score with drastic chords for choir and orchestra. Although nothing even remotely similar had ever occurred in the German city where the premiere was held (not even in earlier historical periods), the audience in Stuttgart was shaken. Writes critic Wolfgang Schreiber: "There must be something in collective memory, that does not have distant Russia as its sole provenance, that lends such power to the music." No one who was at the premiere could eat anything for more than three hours afterward, even though it grew very late.

Phoenix from the Ashes

After the devastating airstrike on Berlin in 1945, the Deutsche Staatsoper was utterly destroyed—except for a single clothes hanger. One of the wardrobe assistants had grabbed the thing as she fled. For decades, the hanger had held expensive evening coats. Among the debris of the smoldering ruins, the firefighters rolled up their hoses. The singers were scattered to the four winds. The day was already dawning.

The enemy's reconnaissance planes, which usually photographed the damage, were expected at midday. Not a single fighter jet was available to drive them off. The German planes (all night fighters) had followed the departing stream of bombers to Holland, and sat scattered across airfields there. They were expected back that evening. The photographs the British Mosquitoes took showed the site of the opera house as just a tiny detail amid the broad swath of destruction. Striking were the city's green spaces, seemingly immune to bombs. The damage assessor Erwin Schäfer, an engineer in the finance ministry's structural engineering department, had been assigned to the fire department's detail. He rejected the assessment of "total loss" for the destroyed opera house, and reasoned as follows: fire walls and a two-story cellar had survived the fire and could be reused. The cellar contained an archive of orchestra scores. In addition, in the period after Giacomo Meyerbeer had taken over directorial duties, the opera had acquired an outstanding reputation. This immaterial value, impervious to destruction by the enemy, must be reckoned along with the material exterior. Also, he said, the ruins—premieres could be held in them on summer nights— were now an especially safe spot, since the strategic Brits never dropped bombs on the same target twice. Finally, he concluded, think of opera praxis itself: all of the things and people that have been destroyed over the course of an opera always reappear at the end of the performance unscathed—they even accept the audience's applause. What's good for the opera, said engineer Schäfer, should be good for its abode. Among his colleagues, Schäfer was considered something of a dreamer.*

War in the Huts

"All operas are about a suspended civil war of the soul." In the fall of 1940, Theodor Adorno and Max Horkheimer were under time pressure. Adorno offered this sentence intuitively. Their research application for the project "Authority and Family" was due at a Columbia University foundation on Monday. It was already Friday.

Neither Horkheimer nor their legal advisor Franz Neumann

---

* In a footnote to his report, Schäfer invoked Venice's opera house, Teatro La Fenice (*fenice* = phoenix, a fabled Egyptian bird that burns to death and then rises, reconstituted, out of its own ashes). It burned down completely three times. And after each fire it became, once again, the site of phenomenal premieres.

liked intuitions much, including the one contained in Adorno's formulation. "It is not," Adorno countered, "that I know something—rather, there is something in me that knows." One can write down a sentence, he said, and then spend one's entire life trying to explain it. If we don't include the sentence as is, he added, we won't be finished by Monday. But his friends, who did not want to talk about opera, only about authority and family, rejected his introductory phrase.

It wasn't until forty-nine years after Adorno's death that a daughter of one of his illegitimate children took up his introductory sentence once more. The issue was still the foundations of capitalism and its more intensive fifth aggregate phase, fascism, "arising from the spirit of families and their struggles." Adorno's descendant was adamant about the sentence, which she had found among his papers and which she wanted to see at least included as an epigraph to a new edition of the work.

Steel mill with blast furnace around 1910. The four English converters are called "rats" or "field rabbits." The one in front is on its back. At the moment it is empty and burning out.

The *Contrat Social* of Families

According to a Shanghai publication, a team of researchers at the University of Giessen has been investigating a remarkable EVOLUTIONARY LEAP that took place either *just before* the development of Homo sapiens, or in the *beginning stages* of the formation of this species. As the first of all animals with souls, as the researchers put it, "children pay back a portion of their production costs to their parents." As a result, the breastfeeding period goes from 5.5 years for apes to just 2.5 years for humans. This developmental leap occurs in a timespan of just 112 generations! From this point on, older siblings start taking care of younger ones.

A reserve army of grandmothers forms. Division of labor by gender, but also between predatory and producing societies. The most striking event, unexplainable by Darwinian categories, say the Chinese, in their report on the Giessen scientists, is the safeguarding of the smooth transfer of experience from generation to generation—though why this is advantageous for reproduction is not at all apparent at first glance.

How is this transfer accomplished? By generations continuing the customs of preceding generations over long periods? Chains of experience and willpower are created, as if by—this is how the Chinese describe it—a COLOSSAL AND WELL-MAINTAINED ORGANIC MACHINE.

It is tempting to conclude from this, adds the economist Ho Wang-Shu, that the difficulties of actually implementing socialism lie in the fact that it in no way represents a *future* goal—in fact, modern (and even industrial!) societies actually evolved out of the crumbling of the PRIMITIVE COOPERATION that defined the sensational career of early humans. That means, the comrade pursued, the works of Marx must be rewritten. The EXCHANGE SOCIETY was derived not from PRIMITIVE ACCU-

MULATION and the concept of the commodity, but from PRIM-
ITIVE FAMILIAL CONTRACTS, as one easily learns, according
to Ho Wang-Shu, from looking at EARLY CHINESE HISTORY.

"Blast Furnaces of the Soul"

The BLAST FURNACES OF THE SOUL work at very different
times than the blast furnaces of industry. Their material comes
from radical forces. Their machinery produces HOT-TEM-
PEREDNESS and ICY COLD, the two energies from which sub-
jectivity arises.

It would be a misunderstanding, said Oskar Negt, to believe
that opera houses themselves, or the arias sung with all the heart's
ardor, are "blast furnaces of the soul." The souls of contemporary
people, that is to say the performers of the musical dramas and
their audiences, have long since been forged. And I don't believe
that they will soften.

He elucidated his remarks as follows:

Medea is used as material in 44 operas.

All 44 operas are based on the tragedy by Euripides.

The tragedy by Euripides is based upon a myth that recounts
the story of Medea.

The terrible (presumably collective) experience that led to the
myth is not known to us.

In this connection Negt quoted a remark made by the opera lover
Sigmund Freud to the composer Alban Berg. The tragedies from
which we infer terrible primordial events are, "without exception,
screen memories." They have shifted from the original occurrence, which is likely present in the soul-lives of both singers and
listeners, to a story that can be told with the aid of music.

It was man, prince of the animals,
Who invented parricide.

But parricide, continued Freud—he had written about it, after all—was not the primordial event, either. If the earth's interior were a time constant, then the smelter from which the "steel of the soul-life" emerges would be equivalent to the glowing magma seventy miles deep under the earth's surface (if, as I've said before, the core were made of liquid time). On this point, he cited a classic:

Why do dogs whine?
They scent from a distance
The spirits' dance.

Medea's Decision

The adventures lay behind them. Where were the aftershocks? After all, feelings take longer to arrive home than ships. Is the fear located in their limbs? Is it hiding? Is it dammed?

The young heroes had shipped out as a united front and come back singly. Jason with the booty. His pursuers still in the wake of his ship. His freshly won mistress—traitor to her country, indispensable means by which he had procured the valuable map (drawn on the lining of a ram's pelt, and now being brought home)—was busy carving her brother into pieces and tossing them bit by bit to their pursuers. (They had brought him along as a hostage.) In the churning darkness of the sea, how were the pursuers to notice the princely flesh, let alone be able to identify it? Left unexplained. At any rate, they veered off.

And then, daily life in Corinth. It didn't take Medea long to realize that she was hated there—she, the foreigner.

Years later. None of Jason's copious promises have been fulfilled. Malicious gossip: Medea, they say, the sorceress from Colchis, has tried to convince Jason's parents to boil their son in a cauldron in the interests of eternal life. The prospect of eternal life *would* certainly have pleased the hero.

In fact, Medea is already doomed. Still no marriage to Jason, the heir apparent. Now she finds out about Jason's plan to marry a princess from Athens. As if she, the woman with whom he has two children, were nothing but air! No one was even going to bother to tell her. She knows that the man who has betrayed her wants to try to win a piece of everlasting life, at least as the father of a dynasty. And so she also knows that the only means she possesses to hurt him is to kill her (and *his*) blooming children.

The Troublesome Sister

In the night before she died (she had helped things along with some poison entrusted to her), Margit prayed, repented, and entertained doubts as to God's benevolence. It was all to do with an occurrence seventy years earlier (but with a prelude many years before that), concerning her first reaction to the bombing death of her dominant sister, Herta. She, the quieter flower, had always stood in the shadows of her superior older sister—the beauty, the merry favorite of both parents, and of all four grandparents. She was the one shown off to relatives and visitors. The life of this bliss-sister was so surrounded by noisy idolatry that Margit, born later, sullenly withdrew, and spurned the few crumbs of attention that did come her way. She became a difficult child, a malcontent, neither boy nor girl, appropriating what affection she could from the free-floating guilt of her parents—they were Protestants, and could find no release for their strife. Some effort was made by the parents to start over with this child—though a nest was never offered that she would want to live in—but the merry sister would burst into the room too precipitously and ruin the fresh start.

So when the message broke upon them that the entire Darmstadt side of their family had been eradicated, Margit was unable to console her parents. She experienced a feeling of relief that frightened her. She was the only one in the household who was able to put what had happened into words.

But she forbade herself any feelings of triumph. So many wounds from her childhood still sought expression in her that she did not forgive her dead sister, but rather aimed the reproaches at herself instead: she would not indulge in any sensation of liberation. This helped the mortgage of guilt that ruled the entire family (except for the dead sister) to accumulate so relentlessly during the course of her lifetime that as the decades passed there was no hope of ever paying it off. The GDR ceased to be. The new freedom of movement (borderless travel!) brought about no reconciliation. She prayed earnestly, sought relief from the feelings she had avoided. But there was never any disposal site available to take them. And so, the disequilibrium from her youth accompanied her literally to her end. Her death was caused not by guilt, but by a revolt in her cells. And since she had no interest in suffering passively, she procured the powerful opiate with which, at 96 years old, she managed to compensate for the *brief joy of 1944*. She declined to feel any remorse.

The Aggressive Gaze of Blood

After their mother's death by fire (which both galleries were forced to watch—usually boisterous, here they found themselves at a loss), Norma's children were brought by an escort to Rome.

Raised in the household of the praetor, their father, possibly they did not believe in the veracity of the event they themselves had witnessed. The two boys, half-Gauls (though in Rome social status is inherited through the father), passed through the senatorial ranks: quaestor, praetor, provincial governor, senator, governor once more, consul, proconsul. At the end of a Roman funeral comes the listing of deeds (*res gestae*). In the course of the ensuing centuries, Norma's grandchildren and great-grandchildren recited the deeds of both her once so faithless lover and all their Roman forefathers extending back to the legendary Ennius. Actors read relevant texts. No word about Norma. The descendants of this branch of the family showed no particular distinction. Had Norma's sacrificial death, which had enabled the rescue of the captive praetor and their children, been worth it, evolutionarily speaking?

Approximately 2,000 years later. A young Swiss federal prosecutor brings down a clan of the 'Ndrangheta that had been entrenched in Winterthur. It turns out that the boss of this mafia organization (which has a global reach) can claim as his ancestor that same praetor who had served in Gaul and been saved by Norma's death. Almost simultaneously it becomes clear that the federal prosecutor, too, is descended from this ancient lineage, but another branch of it. So the death by fire had a late historical consequence, wrested by the firm spirit of the priestess from her martyred body—a body full of rebellion as she burned (one could see her mouth, open for a scream, while the heathens' drumming severed any auditory connection between the spectators and the condemned).

The criminals are sentenced to eighteen years in prison. Two-thirds of the punishment is to be served. The valuable experience of this trial leads the Swiss federal prosecutors' office to make a change in their policy regarding organized crime. In the interests of strengthening the prosecution, they decide that investigation and indictment will be based not on membership in the 'Ndrangheta alone, but on *concrete* acts. That way, there will be fewer acquittals. The successful federal prosecutor and the mafia boss are photographed as their eyes meet over the short distance of the courtroom (a gaze across 2,000 years).

Love as a Hard Laborer

The approximately fifty operas each that Reinhard Keiser and Georg Philipp Telemann wrote for the popular OPER AM GÄNSEMARKT in Hamburg all have a *lieto fine,* an interactive ending that calls upon people to engage in positive life practices. Because one must not fritter away the precious time of the elapsing decades of the Enlightenment by leaving conflicts unresolved, by sowing seeds of doubt, by spreading defeatism and tragic failure.

Sapere aude!

Dare to know—have the courage to use your own understanding. Enjoy watching the collective rational achievement of the singers and orchestra at the end of the opera. In 1740, the critique of "instrumental reason" and "the egocentricity of understanding" had not yet reached maturity. It was neither dogma nor intellectual achievement that sent the galleries of the Gänsemarkt theater into a positive frenzy—and they were who decided on the success of an evening. No, what succeeded was the wit to surprise the audience with an uplifting finale. This final chord, however, had to be preceded by a wave of sadness in the concert hall, a CONCENTRATION OF EMOTION, a TYING OF THE FATAL KNOT OF LIFE, because only then could relief, could rib-expanding joy come in, preparing the audience for the transition from dream to reality (after the end of the piece).

In *Emma and Eginhard*, a seven-hour opera by Telemann,

Charlemagne skulks at night around his palace. (In this he is related to his contemporary, Harun Al-Rashid of Baghdad.) He is on the hunt for any signs of betrayal. He keeps a close eye on his staff. He checks up on his children.

One of his advisors, the learned but not aristocratic Eginhard (modeled on Charlemagne's biographer, Einhard), is having a relationship with the emperor's daughter Emma. The emperor has been spying on the pair. He is an EMPEROR WHO NEVER FORGIVES. In Hamburg's bourgeois theaters, audiences love it when medieval emperors are portrayed as tyrants.

Third act of the opera. Snow has fallen overnight. How can the besotted couple, aware that they have been discovered, flee the fortress? The tracks of a man's shoes in the snow would prove to the emperor that Emma did not spend the night alone. The emperor's daughter invites her beloved to climb onto her shoulders, and carries him off.

By this point, the audience has long since taken the ingenious couple into their hearts. The privy councilor decrees that Eginhard will be arrested. He and Emma will be executed by sword.

Both lovers want to sacrifice themselves—both beg for mercy, each for the other. They would rather die than be parted.

> *When you have won something very dear*
> *and then must lose it,*
> *grieving is necessary.*
> *Mourning enriches;*
> *denial impoverishes.*

The opera house falls silent. For the scene in which everyone awaits the couple's execution, Telemann wrote a largo. It is performed by the deep string instruments, accompanied by tympani. The audience at the Gänsemarkt opera peers into an abyss.

It is only after such an experience that happiness is worth anything. Jubilation after the final chorus. Everyone loves the delicate, leptosome chronicler and scribe Eginhard, a thin slice of a man who fits well on the shoulders of his corpulent girlfriend. It's obvious that the thunder-thighed emperor with his powerful shoulders is related to this young woman (he will eventually die of high blood pressure and obesity, when his heart-pump can no longer supply his massive body). So how could he possibly cut off her head? He should honor the feat of her feet in the snow! Love is hard labor. Music softens the rigidity in the emperor's head: he changes his mind.

Flu at the Opera

In February 2015, it sent the most robust managers straight to bed. At 5 a.m., CEO Frank H. signaled his assistant's computer that he was at home wrapped in blankets, and that she should cancel all appointments; she got to the office only at 8 a.m. and found the message then. The flu shot developed for the winter of 2015 had failed. The germs that appeared were not the ones they had expected, and the microbial participants of this subculture took advantage of the unusual scale of the attack surface. Particularly disastrous was the situation of the great opera stages in the southern part of the republic. In an opera house, one can regulate neither the draftiness nor the amount of people with whom one comes into contact.

The Original Form of Opera

In the eleventh century, Europe's capital is in Provence (Rome is in ruins, Aachen abandoned, Byzantium far away). It is a populated countryside, not a single town. At night—we have to re-

member it was warmer than today—the inhabitants come together. They tell stories. Then they sing. Then they tell stories
again. Under the stars.

The trained kolkhoz engineer Arkady Trifonov is writing a
study about this receptacle of original, i.e., oral literature. Although he only speaks broken French, he has turned to a collection of the *chantefables* of the period, the early medieval stories
with music. Trifonov lost his research in his home country and
settled amidst the granite ruins of an old castle, the remaining
stones of a castrum within sight of the Mediterranean (he grows
bay leaves and sells wreaths of them in the port of Marseilles). He
knows all the Romance scholars at the universities in the south
of France. They are working their way toward the man with the
beard. Trifonov is a reconstructionist—an artistic movement of
great historical merit.

A New Type of Opera in Vienna

The young director had come to prominence through a rapid
succession of productions in the metropolises of Central Europe.
In Vienna she was considered a star. Currently she was directing
an operatic version of Sophocles' *Antigone*.

At the moment, her most precious possession was the child in
its eighth month residing in her womb. That was the best thing
she was able to bring to the production. As image and as sound.
Her heartbeat was also something she thought of as wholly her
own. And so, both the child and her heart were to set the tone for
the play's immortal texts. The props department had gotten hold
of an ultrasound device. Into this installation for two visual and
acoustic voices, the director, who was also an actress and a singer,
embedded Sophocles' text, as well as fragments from Deleuze
and Guattari's *Anti-Oedipus*, which she herself performed. In

the ultrasound projected onto the back wall of the stage, her son could be seen moving around energetically. This, said the artist, is a contemporary opera.

Such a production ought not to drag on. And for me, it was a once-in-a-lifetime installation. I think that for superstitious reasons alone I would never, after the successful birth of my son, be able to repeat such a CONCERT OF LIVING FORCES. As a radical and as a modern artist I won't repeat anything, anyway.

The young director was Polish. The performance took place in Vienna. Audiences were delighted. The accompanist hardly even got to play the piano. He did play a longer loop from the overture to the second act of Verdi's *Il Corsaro*. The soft music prepared a bed for the sonic and visual text event.

Plato's Ban on Music

The classicist Wülfing-von Martitz notes that in his *Politeia*, Plato, in contrast to the Pythagoreans, wants to do away with music entirely. Music lulls *thumos*.

In nourishment (farmers)

In armament (warriors)

In enlightenment (philosophers)

Therefore, music is detrimental to all three relevant sectors of concrete praxis. The senses and the intellect must not be allowed to "wallow" in dreaminess like cattle in a quagmire.

Lost Sketch by John Cage

During the final rehearsals for his *Europeras* 1 & 2 at the Frankfurt opera house in the autumn of 1987, John Cage was staying at the Hotel Frankfurter Hof. This meant that, when he received the disturbing news that the opera house was on fire, he didn't have far to hurry to the scene. He took a tape recorder with him, and he had filled the pockets of his winter overcoat with various different kinds of special microphones. Frankfurt's fire brigade had several of its units ready for an assault on the stage area, the center of the fire. By now a firestorm had already developed in this part of the opera house. It was simply too dangerous to send in the fire teams against it. They would have to let the fire burn.

It was only after the roof fell in, bringing a mass of building material down with it, that parts of the fire could be put out. Cage found that the acoustic power of a firestorm of this kind produced a sound he'd never heard before: an "infernal hissing." When he asked the fire chiefs about it, they explained that the sound was produced by the flames sucking the oxygen out of the surrounding air. A continuous noise could be heard on the tapes Cage used to record the sounds (he listened to them immediately afterwards, but the recording did not correspond to what he'd heard at the scene). He played it several times to other people present, including to members of the orchestra who were now appearing at the scene of the inferno. Cage had also recorded the high-pitched tone of the firemen's voices, caused by excitement and nervous strain, and the same phenomenon among several of the spectators.

In the days that followed, before the first performance of his two *Europeras*, which had now been postponed until December 12, Cage acquired an audiotape from a sound technician at Hessischer Rundfunk containing recordings of the discharge and impact of shells fired from British twelve-pounders, a type of heavy artillery. On the night before the premiere of his operas (the performance had been moved to Frankfurt's main theater), Cage packed his audiotapes and notes into a cardboard box. It contained the draft for his "Suite for Cacophony and Orchestra," known as *Europera* 2a. Using the material he'd recorded at the opera house fire, Cage had tried to set to sounds the image of an air attack on Beirut. Along with the noises of the shell explosions (which he'd got from Hessischer Rundfunk) and the sounds of the fire at the opera house, Cage had included a passage from the last act of Bernd Alois Zimmermann's opera *The Soldiers* (containing no vocal music), and a page of sheet music that he'd sketched out in rough and which the members of the orchestra were to play on instruments of their own choosing according to a principle of random determination. This package, unmarked and unprofessionally tied together, was mistaken for rubbish by the hotel's chambermaid and thrown in the bin: lost sketch for sound and orchestra by John Cage.

Snot and Water

Shortly before his death, John Cage put together another package that has survived and whose content was recently made the subject of a performance by Heiner Goebbels in Baden-Baden. Following a long telephone conversation with his partner, who had caught the gruesome March flu that was raging along the east coast of the United States, Cage wrote his "Short Concerto for Cough (Deep in the Bronchials), Sniffling and Selected Notes by Bach, Schönberg and Myself." The notes form an aleatory input, a kind of meal to which the soloists of the Ensemble Modern help themselves; their organized sound jostling with the breaks of something completely different, namely the sounds made by the body when seized with the coughs and irritations of a cold. Cage claimed that nowhere else was there anything richer in variations than this forcing of the air from the stomach through the vocal folds and on into the head, accompanied by the bronchial tubes. It was, according to him, superior to the voices of opera singers. It had, he added, significantly more harmonics. Following a trans-Atlantic telephone call with his close friend Heinz-Klaus Metzger, he gave the piece the German title "Rotz und Wasser"—"Snot and Water."

"Infiltration of a Love"

Near the end of the war, in a manor house crowded with fugitive relatives and strangers, a powerful sense of abandon took hold. Observers and close friends recognized this abandon as love.

"Love": what a conventional term for an entangled system of self-abandonment and personal transformation. A desperate couple showed up at the house—and the naked passion with which they focused on each other caused Fritzi von Schaake, that very same evening, to fall in love with her cousin, a lieutenant. The following day, the heiress of a neighboring estate living in one of the house's garrets left her husband. She had long railed against the prison of her marriage; it only took witnessing one example to trigger her decision. In the west wing of the house, a group of girls from the same graduating class in Breslau—up to that point an inconspicuous bunch who had been trained for the future in Czechoslovakian camps, and were now on the run—were seized by a kind of bacchanalian compulsion, an urge to celebrate life, an obsession with surrender. No one wanted to be alone anymore. They had plenty of options. When faced with imminent redeployment to one of the fronts—which made death foreseeable—young soldiers sought explosions of experience in the brevity of life. They had nothing more to lose. In a fit of decisiveness, the cousin who had been infected at the very beginning of the love infiltration shot her freshly acquired lover to death, and then herself. No doctors or vaccine against the epidemic anywhere in the vicinity. Let one more person try to tell me that "love" (whatever it might be), isn't collective, isn't contagious.

"Oh My Heart, this Thunder-Sheet"

After the taxi deposited me outside the emergency room at the last minute—speechless with pain in my arm, an urgent need to vomit the whole way, an ineffable feeling of failing—the diagnosis of a heart attack destroyed any illusions I might have had about the immortality of my body (up until that point, I had not seen the symptoms adding up to any whole). Afterward, well-rested, swathed in white, and connected to various machines, I regained trust in my circulation. Now, constantly vexed, I look at my body as at a foreign entity, a culprit. I don't take many risks. But as an opera singer, for the sake of my career I have to wager my life on a daily basis.

My voice's specialty is "high French tenor," an art form that has nearly died out on the WORLD'S GREAT STAGES. Meyerbeer, Rossini, Auber, and all the repertoire of heartfelt pap from nineteenth-century French demi-opera. I hope Mark Andre will write a new part for me.

The warmheartedness in the vibrations of my vocal cords, something like a very high trumpet, requires not only lung power; in fact it seems to me that with each outburst of passion I give off tiny quanta of my being, so that if I sing like that—out of temperament, out of ardor—many thousands of times, I will have totally transformed my body into expressiveness. The sources of song are reserves of air in the lower lungs, but I seem to also have air sacs in my intestinal region that I use for backup. Where others digest, I lift up my high notes.

This "marvel of emotional stimulation," as a New York critic called it, has nothing to do with the conventional muscle we call the "heart," and therefore it is not affected by my decreased hopes for the continuance of that muscle in the left side of my chest. And so, what gets transmitted to my listeners is not "heart's blood" (as that generous critic claimed), but an emission from my lungs and throat shored up by my intestines, a keen puff that sweeps along my vocal cords and that comprises the entirety of my life-sap. I call it—in contrast to that fickle, holey SPONGE (my physical heart) that drives the blood through my body—my THUNDER-SHEET. It is a heart in the spiritual sense. Rossini wrote his coloraturas for it—for example, an aria that practically has my name on it, the aria of Arnold, a Swiss mercenary captain in love who has nothing urgent to do with the historical plot of *William Tell*, a purpose-free and thought-free flight of mind with four high Fs: an "enclave of pure music" in Rossini's final opera (often borrowed for other works of the maestro's). I call this "magic of the rarefied heights" an INLAY FOR STAGE, THUNDER-SHEET, AND ORCHESTRA.

Composed more than one hundred years ago just for me. I had my performance—a "celestial volcano spewing from above— from the heavens down to earth" (and it is not lava that it is dispensing)—digitally recorded with the highest quality equipment, so that my true heart, my thunder-sheet, will keep beating long after I have ceased to be.

The silly muscle to the left under my throat remains a quitter. I often talk to it, entice it like a dog that has grown sluggish, throw sticks for it, pet it—all to keep it willing for a little while longer.

On my calendar are upcoming appearances in Buenos Aires, Singapore, Oslo, Cottbus, Pferdsinnig an der Elster, at the State Opera House in Berlin, in Zurich, at Angkor Wat (an open-air performance), and in Adelaide. I'd definitely like to hang on for all of them, as long as my vocal cords will bear the sounds.

New Directions Paperbooks — a partial listing

Martín Adán, The Cardboard House
César Aira, Ema, the Captive
  An Episode in the Life of a Landscape Painter
  Ghosts
Will Alexander, The Sri Lankan Loxodrome
Paul Auster, The Red Notebook
Honoré de Balzac, Colonel Chabert
Djuna Barnes, Nightwood
Charles Baudelaire, The Flowers of Evil*
Bei Dao, City Gate, Open Up
Nina Berberova, The Ladies From St. Petersburg
Max Blecher, Adventures in Immediate Irreality
Roberto Bolaño, By Night in Chile
  Distant Star
  Last Evenings on Earth
  Nazi Literature in the Americas
Jorge Luis Borges, Labyrinths
  Professor Borges
  Seven Nights
Coral Bracho, Firefly Under the Tongue*
Kamau Brathwaite, Ancestors
Basil Bunting, Complete Poems
Anne Carson, Antigonick
  Glass, Irony & God
Horacio Castellanos Moya, Senselessness
Louis-Ferdinand Céline
  Death on the Installment Plan
  Journey to the End of the Night
Rafael Chirbes, On the Edge
Inger Christensen, alphabet
Jean Cocteau, The Holy Terrors
Peter Cole, The Invention of Influence
Julio Cortázar, Cronopios & Famas
Albert Cossery, The Colors of Infamy
Robert Creeley, If I Were Writing This
Guy Davenport, 7 Greeks
Osamu Dazai, No Longer Human
H.D., Tribute to Freud
  Trilogy
Helen DeWitt, The Last Samurai
Robert Duncan, Selected Poems
Eça de Queirós, The Maias
William Empson, 7 Types of Ambiguity
Shusaku Endo, Deep River
Jenny Erpenbeck, The End of Days
  Visitation
Lawrence Ferlinghetti
  A Coney Island of the Mind

F. Scott Fitzgerald, The Crack-Up
  On Booze
Forrest Gander, The Trace
Henry Green, Pack My Bag
Allen Grossman, Descartes' Loneliness
John Hawkes, Travesty
Felisberto Hernández, Piano Stories
Hermann Hesse, Siddhartha
Takashi Hiraide, The Guest Cat
Yoel Hoffman, Moods
Susan Howe, My Emily Dickinson
  That This
Bohumil Hrabal, I Served the King of England
Sonallah Ibrahim, That Smell
Christopher Isherwood, The Berlin Stories
Fleur Jaeggy, Sweet Days of Discipline
Alfred Jarry, Ubu Roi
B.S. Johnson, House Mother Normal
James Joyce, Stephen Hero
Franz Kafka, Amerika: The Man Who Disappeared
John Keene, Counternarratives
Laszlo Krasznahorkai, Satantango
  The Melancholy of Resistance
  Seiobo There Below
Eka Kurniawan, Beauty Is a Wound
Rachel Kushner, The Strange Case of Rachel K
Mme. de Lafayette, The Princess of Clèves
Lautréamont, Maldoror
Sylvia Legris, The Hideous Hidden
Denise Levertov, Selected Poems
Li Po, Selected Poems
Clarice Lispector, The Hour of the Star
  Near to the Wild Heart
  The Passion According to G. H.
Federico García Lorca, Selected Poems*
  Three Tragedies
Nathaniel Mackey, Splay Anthem
Stéphane Mallarmé, Selected Poetry and Prose*
Norman Manea, Captives
Javier Marías, Your Face Tomorrow (3 volumes)
Bernadette Mayer, Works & Days
Thomas Merton, New Seeds of Contemplation
  The Way of Chuang Tzu
Henri Michaux, Selected Writings
Dunya Mikhail, The War Works Hard
Henry Miller, The Colossus of Maroussi
  Big Sur & The Oranges of Hieronymus Bosch

*BILINGUAL EDITION

For a complete listing, request a free catalog from New Directions, 80 8th Avenue, New York, NY 10011
or visit us online at ndbooks.com